Head Over Heart

Mara A. Miller

No part of this book may be reproduced or transmitted in any form or by any means, electronic or mechanical, including photocopying, recording, or by any information storage and retrieval system without the written permission of the author, except where permitted by law.

This book is a work of fiction. Names, characters, places, and incidents either are products of the author's imagination are used fictitiously. Any resemblance to actual persons, living or dead, events, or locales is entirely coincidental.

Book cover designed by Kellie Dennis:
http://www.bookcoverbydesign.co.uk/

Copyright © 2015 Mara A. Miller

All rights reserved.

ISBN: 1514225832
ISBN-13: 978-1514225837

Other Works

All This Time (A Kindle Worlds Story)
Cheap Guitars (Cheap Series 1)
Head Over Hoof (Over Series 1)
!

ACKNOWLEDGMENTS

I need to give a huge shout out to my editors, Amanda Higgins and Laura Goodfellow. You girls put up with so much whining, it's unbelievable... even when I had the novel nearly finished three months ago and decided to completely rewrite it. You girls are so much more than friends or editors... you're my soundboards, my sanity, the kick in the ass to get me writing again when you're eager to read more.

Thanks to my Facebook friends, too, who have put up with an unbelievable amount of status updates when I'm procrastinating. :P Thanks also to Kate who was my cheerleader at the beginning of writing this, and most of all to Kendra, who waited *so* patiently for this book.. Also, thanks to my evil fairy godmother for the autocrit subscription! Being an Indie author isn't easy and I'm so thankful for the help I've had along the way.

I also can't finish these acknowledgements without thanking the wonderful Kellie Dennis for the cover. As always, you've done a beautiful job!

For Kendra

You've waited *so* patiently for this book! Love you, girl! Don't deafen Aaron or the kids when you get a copy!

Chapter One

Briana

Three Weeks Ago

I stopped midway down the gravel driveway. Had I decided to take my brother back up to Kentucky? Was I so scared I didn't see any other option?

Giving into the urge to run usually resulted in getting nowhere fast...and I ran like a weak, pathetic coward.

No, I told myself. I refused to admit I ran.

It's *Thanksgiving*. It's reasonable to go visit Evie in Kentucky. A last minute road trip made the perfect solution.

With a lot of decisions to make in a short period, I needed to take myself away from a situation that could have gotten crazy very fast. I didn't... I *wasn't* sure how Aidan would react when and if I told him he got me *pregnant*. Cynthia terminated a pregnancy a year ago. She still felt the fresh pain of the abortion. What if Aidan felt the same way? Aidan couldn't know about my baby yet. I needed the time to process the information myself. I rested my head against the steering wheel and sighed heavily.

Nope.

I ran.

Definitely ran.

Might as well call me *chicken*.

What happened to focusing on college and not getting distracted? I rubbed my still-flat stomach and sighed. A lot of good *that* did.

Lora had no idea where we went. I picked up my phone, aware the screen would be riddled with text and missed call notifications. Ten calls in total; three from Lora, two from Cynthia, one from Nikki, and four from Aidan. I rejected the call as soon as my screen lit up, not sure I could talk to him so soon, even if I wanted to. Maybe I wasn't being fair but I didn't need to be fair in this situation. I had no idea what he would think or say, but in the back of my mind all I could remember was Cynthia telling me about the baby she almost had with him. I needed time to process everything that happened after I fell off Blue Moon, and even more so after Cynthia and Aberlie ganged up on me with the pregnancy test.

I ached all over. Falling off a horse sucked.

"Suck it up, Buttercup," I said to myself, "Everything will be fine."

My brother stretched in his seat beside me and yawned loudly.

"Are we at Evie's yet?"

I rubbed the tears out of my eyes. "We're almost there. I needed to stop driving for a minute."

"You're not okay, are you?"

Kevin reached over and rubbed my shoulder.

"I'm not," I said, "but I will be."

"Are you freaking out because you're pregnant?"

"Yeah..."

"Well, dumbass, that's what you get for not abstaining."

I snorted, sat up a little straighter and playfully slapped at his arm. "Please don't tell me they're teaching you in that high school."

"What? I have permission to—"

I gagged. Actually gagged at the thought of my brother having sex.

"Ugh, I so didn't need that image, Kevin!"

He burst into laughter. "I got you to stop whining though, didn't I?"

I glared at him, but my tiny smile grew wider when he childishly stuck out his tongue.

"You're awful," I said, "and act like a two year old sometimes."

"That's not true," he shot back, yawning. "What's the time?"

I put my car back into drive and maneuvered onto the driveway. "I'm not sure. Like five?"

"Evie is going to kill us."

"She'll be happy to see us. She always gets up this early, since she needs to feed her horses."

"So you *think*," Kevin said.

I rolled my eyes. "What's got you in a good mood?"

Kevin shrugged.

My phone buzzed, signaling another text message. I gave in.

> Me: I'm fine. Stop freaking out.
> Nikki: Where are you!?
> Me: I can't talk right now. I'll get back to you.

She sent me another text but I turned off my phone before I became tempted to read it. Nikki would try to talk sense into me; would want to hear every detail she missed. I couldn't. My hands already shook every time I thought about what happened.

"Did I wake you up?" I finally said to shake myself out of my own thoughts.

"Well, you're kind of loud when you start crying and talking to yourself." He pressed a hand against my forehead. "Are you sure falling off Blue Moon didn't make you go crazy? Did you bang your head against something?"

"Okay, *seriously*, I'm starting to wonder if Mom or Dad dropped you when you were a baby." I laughed.

"Can we go to the graveyard?" He turned his head to stare out of the window.

I sucked in a deep breath. I hadn't expected the question. I *never* thought about it. In fact, I completely planned on ignoring the fact that my parents were dead and buried in the ground somewhere in Nicholasville, not far from our old house. Mom always had a strange thing about living next to graveyards.

"U-um," I said. "Y-yeah of course we can."

"If it'll be too hard on you them we don't need to, Kevin said.

"No...No, Kev. We can go. I think it might be good for the both of us."

"I do too."

He was on a real smartass roll this morning. I decided to let it slide. What else could I have done when he asked me the question? Tell him no to going to see our parents' grave? What kind of example would I be setting for him?

There I went, over-thinking *everything*. That's why I was in my car at that moment with my brother on a trip to see an old family friend I hadn't talked to in months.

"Cool," he said. "It would be nice to leave some flowers for Mom. You're not allowed to be gloomy and mopey, though."

"I'm am not!"

Kevin scowled. "Then what is it you're doing right now?"

"I—" I started, not sure what to say to him. I wasn't projecting my feelings too openly, was I? I tried to think of myself as the type of person who was good at hiding my emotions.

"Seriously, Bri?! It's Thanksgiving. Mom and Dad wouldn't want us to be sad about anything."

I sighed. "All right. No glooming or moping. We'll see Mom and Dad, drink some coffee and sit and talk to them a while."

Kevin beamed. "Sounds like a nice family outing."

I glared. "Seriously?"

"What? Come on, you can't tell me I'm not allowed to joke once in a while."

I sighed, relenting *again*. I needed to stop giving into him so much but at the same time I wanted to avoid the argument that would happen if I kept on trying to rain on Kevin's parade. He was in a good mood—probably because we were in Kentucky—and I didn't want it to change.

"You never answered my question."

"Huh?" I asked.

"About Aidan. When are you going to tell him you're pregnant?"

I almost—*almost*—told him to drop the subject. It made me freak out thinking about it. I didn't want to be pregnant but I didn't not want to keep the baby *either*. I got myself into this situation and now a new human would be depending on me. It was time I pulled up my big girl panties and dealt with it.

Did that include telling Aidan he would be a father soon?

"I'm not sure."

I'm a chicken shit.

~*~

I sat on porch swing, my heart pounding in my chest by the time seven o'clock rolled around.

"I really am sorry about that, Bri," Evie said, balancing a cigarette, two cups of coffee, and a plate of food in the other.

She pulled her shot gun on us.

"It's okay. I know I should have called first."

I gratefully took the plate. It had a full scatter of biscuits and gravy, eggs, and bacon. Kevin skipped breakfast, and chose to go to bed instead. "I thought you sold that car," she said, pointing to the light blue vehicle.

"I did," I said. "Lora bought it back for me."

"That's sweet of her. She taking over the payments for you?"

"Well, I didn't stick around long enough to find out if that was what she wanted to do when she got it back for me. I kind of..."

I didn't know what to say, so I huffed, shook my head, and looked down at my plate.

"You weren't sure what to do, were you?"

I said nothing. Instead I took a messy bite of my breakfast, egg yolk dribbling down my chin.

"I know you ran. You're just like your mother." Evie laughed. "You know she almost left your father after she found out she was pregnant with you?"

I stopped mid-chew, jaw slack. I tried to say, "*Pregnant?* What do you mean?" but it came out in a garbled mess. Evie laughed harder and took a step away from me so she could draw a drag off her cigarette.

"Lora called while I made you breakfast."

I swallowed my food. "Oh," I said. "I guess you know then."

"You were always such a careful girl, Briana. What happened?"

I squeezed my lips together tightly, sucked air into my mouth, and held it there until my cheeks hurt before I released it in a heavy sigh. "Honestly? I don't know what happened. I don't know what being a 'careful girl' has to do with me getting pregnant, either."

"Well I hope you understand some of what—"

"*No*," I said, shaking my head. "*Obviously* I know what happened. I mean that I don't know what the heck happened with Aidan... I didn't think I would ever see him that way."

A few more puffs on her cigarette. She squeezed her eyebrows together in thought, then threw the cigarette to the ground and put it out with the tip of her boots.

"It's easy to get so tangled up in your emotions for a man that you won't realize it's a mistake until it's too late."

"I'm not in love with him."

"I never said you're in love with him." Evie took a pull on her cigarette. "You're the one jumping to that conclusion."

I rolled my eyes, deciding to ignore the love issue all together. "I'll admit sleeping with him wasn't a mistake."

"Lora told me he had a girlfriend," I said.

Evie would never judge someone but disappointment clearly etched itself along the edges of her frown.

"It still wasn't a mistake."

I wasn't sure who I tried convincing with that statement.

"Are you going to tell him?"

"Why does everyone keep asking me that question? I'm sick of hearing it. I need to tell him. I know, but I will when I'm ready."

The swing rocked back when Evie sat down on it. I grabbed my plate so I wouldn't drop it then pulled both my legs up on the swing and crossed them.

"I'm not saying you need to rush into anything," Evie said. "You're an adult, you can make your own choices."

"I know that," I said. "I'm just not sure if I am even going back to school... or to Tennessee for that matter."

"You're running away from your problems, sweetie."

"Why should I go back? I don't think Kevin was very happy in Tennessee."

"Briana, you and I both know that boy. He's unhappy if you don't cook his steak right. This isn't about Kevin. It's about *you*."

I sighed, and dove into the explanation. I told Evie everything—how Kevin couldn't live with me while I went to college. I found Cynthia in a roommate ad on Facebook, and how she introduced me to Aidan as her boyfriend yet I still found her having sex with his cousin, Lee. I vented about how complicated Cyn and Aidan were even though I found it impossible to say no to him once we became romantically involved.

"I care about Aidan, Evie. I *really* do. I'm just worried that he'll tell me not to keep this baby. Cynthia told me she had an abortion a year ago right after I fell off his horse. She ganged up on me with Aidan's mother so I would take a pregnancy test. That's how I found out. I didn't stick around long after that. I just... It was like my fight or flight instincts kicked in, in that moment, and I felt like I had to do something immediately to change my situation for me, Kevin, and the baby. I love Lora dearly but she's not the best person to leave my brother alone with. I overreacted when I decided to drive up here but I also feel like I haven't been the best parent to my brother, so how can I be a good mom to this baby if I can't admit that I made a mistake leaving Kentucky in the first place? That I have to rely on someone else to take care of my brother?"

Annoyed, I wiped some tears from my face after I got done purging. That's what I did. I purged. There's no other word to describe it.

Evie sighed heavily. "You've been through so much since your parents died, bless your heart."

I half laughed, half scoffed. "No shit."

I squeaked and covered my mouth but Evie only laughed at me.

"But you also need help and you need to be able to admit that to yourself," she said.

I didn't say anything because I didn't know what to say to her. She had a point. I just wasn't sure if it was a point I wanted to take seriously.

"Look, I'm more than happy for you to stay here until after Thanksgiving. You need to figure things out."

"I do," I said, nodding in agreement.

"But I think you need to call your friends and let them know what's going on. Lora said your friend, Nikki, has been worrying for you like crazy. The only reason Lora even mentioned Aidan was that he showed up at her house looking for you."

Oh, *God*, I thought to myself, shrinking into the porch swing a little more.

~*~

Aidan

"That dog has got to go," Mom said, pointing her hand frantically at the black and white Border collie, one hand cradling a spot her spine where Daisy knocked her back into the counter.

"Aw, come on Aunt Abs, Daisy ain't doing nothing wrong. We've kept her cooped up in here so long she's starting to go stir crazy. I need to take her outside on a leash. It's fucking ridiculous," said Lee.

Cynthia groaned next to me.

"They keep having this fight," she said.

I gritted my teeth. Lee wouldn't listen to anyone about his dog. Not even the huge bruise on his face deterred him from keeping her.

"You should get rid of the damn dog, Lee," I bit out.

"Fuck you, Aidan."

He bent down to rub her chest. Daisy ate up the attention, the *thump thump thump* of her tail unnerving Mom's rabbit to the point of stamping his foot against his cage.

I flexed my fists since I had half a mind to punch him again.

Briana disappeared. Everyone refused to tell me where she went. Nikki told me Briana moved to Kentucky, but I heard nothing after that. Lora wasn't too far of a drive away from us so the thought crossed my mind a few times to drive out there to see if she would talk to me. It's possible Nikki lied. Maybe Bri went to her aunt's.

"We should let them fight this out," Cynthia said. "You know he won't listen to you."

"You're part of the reason I have no idea where Briana is, asshole. It's your fault she ever fell off Blue. If you would've kept Daisy tied up or in the house like me and Mom kept telling you I wouldn't be wondering where the hell Bri went."

"Don't you dare put that on me," Lee bit out. "Briana acted scared of her own shadow."

"Like hell she did," I bit out.

I continuously told myself, until that moment, it wasn't worth it to fight with my cousin over what happened. I couldn't stand it anymore. I flexed my fists, the temptation to punch him getting stronger.

"I don't want to hear your shit anyway. You were too busy fucking Bri to care about Cynthia."

"Okay," Cyn said, stepping between the two of us quickly. "That's enough. Aidan and I made a mutual decision to break up, Lee."

"It didn't seem like it when you cried your eyes out the other night," Lee said.

I looked at Cynthia, surprised. She cried?

"Now listen, you two," Mom said, putting her hands on her waist. "I don't care for you starting a pissing contest in my kitchen. Lee, your damn dog has to go."

"Well, maybe I'll move out."

"Up to you, son, but I'm not having Daisy here anymore. She's a dog who I can't trust around my horses *and* I can't afford it. I sure as hell won't have a dog who chases my rabbit, either."

The rabbit picked up his food dish and threw it against the bars of his cage, displeased Mom put him in there to protect him from Daisy. Daisy ran around like a wild, uncontrollable animal and Lee laughed about it most of the time. I don't even think he cared too much about what happened with Briana.

Again, I considered punching Lee in the face, if nothing else than to prove my point. His fucking dog needed to go. It became harder by the second to contain my anger.

"You go ahead and do that."

Cyn rolled her eyes. "Okay, enough. Why don't I keep Daisy for a while?"

"Are you nuts?" I asked Cyn. "Daisy is destructive as hell. She destroyed my old book case last week. Why would you subject yourself to that torture?"

"I don't know why you give a shit about a book case," Lee said. "You don't live here anymore. I do."

"*Bottom line*," Mom said, raising her voice to prevent us from arguing, "Daisy is destructive and she needs to go. You know as well as I do that we want to help animals but sometimes they need to be rehomed."

"This is bullshit." Lee stormed past us, whistling for Daisy. She trotted after him with a little tail wag like she didn't have a care in the world.

"It's not her fault," Cyn said. "She needs obedience training."

Mom and I looked at each other.

"I don't care if he adopted her from a shelter. We've been re-homing animals for years, it won't hurt us to re-home another one. Daisy should be on a sheep farm."

"Come on..." Cyn said, finally speaking up. "I really think if Lee just spent more time with her that she wouldn't be as bad."

"Whatever," I said, digging my car keys out of my back pocket. "I'm out of here. I need to run a few errands. Call me if you need anything."

"Oh," Cyn said. "Well, guess I'll see you later."

There it was—the awkwardness that developed around us since we broke up. I tried not to notice it but it was hard.

"Would you mind dropping some mail off for me?" Mom asked.

"Yeah, sure thing," I said.

"Great, it's on the table near the door. Get it on your way out." Mom spared no second glance to me.

I was certain things would get less awkward between me and Cyn eventually. She and Mom started acting weird a week ago, like they knew something I didn't, but I sure wasn't going to get an answer from anyone. I didn't plan on really running errands. Lora had to know where Bri was and I planned on getting her to tell me. Eventually someone would have to tell me. They couldn't keep me in the dark.

"Actually, do you mind if I come with you?" Cyn said, stopping me on the way out of the house. She beat me to grabbing Mom's mail. "I need a ride to Bobby's clinic."

"Ask Lee to do it," I said, taking the mail from her.

"He's pouting right now about your mom making him get rid of the dog," she said. "I doubt he'll want to drive me anywhere."

"Where's your car?"

Cynthia sighed, brushing her hair out of her face. "I'm letting Mom borrow it for the day."

"Oh," I said. Cynthia followed me to the car. "How is your mother doing?"

"With the divorce? Awful, but Dad is a dick anyway."

I sighed. I really didn't want to give her a ride. Cynthia got in the Nova and shut the door, signifying that she wasn't in the mood to listen.

We stayed quiet after that. The thought of her crying the other night bothered the hell out of me. I wanted to ask her, but I wasn't sure how. Opening that can of worms again might be a bad idea. Cynthia and I were a good couple once but we became toxic to each other toward the end of it.

"Lee was being a dick," Cyn said.

"Huh?" I said.

"Earlier? When he told you I cried? He was being a dick."

"*Did* you cry?"

"I'm under a lot of stress."

"We aren't good for each other anymore, Cyn."

Cynthia glanced at me then turned her head quickly. "I know," she said. "But it doesn't mean I don't miss you sometimes."

"Cyn, I can't."

"I know, Aidan...I know."

Chapter Two

Briana

Kevin still wanted to see our parents. That's why, two days before Thanksgiving, I carried a couple of blankets, a bucket of fried chicken, and bouquet of flowers for Mom in my arms. Kevin refused to help me.

"Hey Mom..." I said when we found her grave. Our parents were buried next to each other. They had one big headstone with an epitaph that sucked now that I stared at it.

For Mom and Dad. They were taken too soon.

It sucked but I couldn't afford something better.

"Hey Daddy..." I said, sitting down, afraid to touch the tombstone.

Kevin sat down next to me, rustling leaves and twigs with a loud, heavy sigh.

"Your baby is okay, right?" He asked. We decided to come to the graveyard after my follow-up appointment; a check-up, to make sure things were okay after falling off Blue Moon. "Cause this is a crappy place to tell me it's not okay."

I rolled my eyes. "The baby is fine. I told you that, right? Everything is on track, including my awful morning sickness and sore breasts."

"TMI!"

I grinned. "You asked."

"This sucks." Kevin glanced at our parents' tombstone. "Can I have some chicken?"

I rolled my eyes despite myself and handed him the box. I didn't want to think too much about being eight weeks pregnant. Instead, I wanted to focus on visiting Mom and Dad's grave.

We hadn't talked about our parents dying in a while. I think we would always grieve for them...It's hard get over the death of a loved one, let alone two, when they're taken from you without warning. I missed Mom. I stared at her grave, hugging myself in one of her old t-shirts. I used to think she would be there for me when I decided to start a family. I wanted—no...*needed*—to talk to her. If I focused hard and took in a deep enough breath, I could still smell her old perfume through my coat. I refused to wash it.

I placed the flowers in front of their grave and grabbed a piece of chicken.

"Shouldn't we avoid poultry until Thanksgiving?" Kevin mused.

"The chicken shack is quicker. Besides, poultry is better than beef."

"Are you always going to be a health nut?"

"I am not a health nut," I said. "This wouldn't be fried if I otherwise."

"You're weirder since you found out you're pregnant. Oh, yeah, in case you didn't know..." He tried his hardest to sound serious even though he laughed. "Mom and Dad, Bri got knocked up."

"Kevin!" I yelped, smacking him on the arm. "Ow!"

We glared at each other for a moment. We never erupted into full on sibling fights anymore, but old habits are hard to kick. For a moment, I forgot I needed to be the mature one and stuck my tongue out at him.

"Dad would *kill* you if he was alive right now," Kevin said.

"What do you think about moving back to Kentucky?" I asked instead, ignoring him.

I seriously contemplated moving back to Kentucky. I couldn't shake the feeling we needed to move home. Nothing wouldn't be right until I did, I was certain of it.

My timing could have been better.

"What am I supposed to do about school if we move back?" Kevin asked, spitting out a piece of chicken he put into his mouth.

"What do you care about school? I thought you hated the high school Lora put you in."

"It's weird with her being a teacher there, but it hasn't been bad."

I wrapped a blanket around my shoulders. It was cold, but not cold enough that I needed to bundle up with a hat and scarf. I liked the weather in Kentucky for that reason... unless it got hit by arctic wind chills. That sucked more than I could ever express with words.

"I think moving back might be good for us both."

"I think the idea sucks," Kevin said.

"What caused big change in heart?"

Kevin focused his eyes anywhere he could but at me. I forgot about eating to stare at him.

He squirmed. "Quit staring at me."

"Why? Is there something you're not telling me?"

"Can we go eat in the car? This is weird. It was a stupid idea to come and eat over Mom and Dad's grave."

Kevin stood up, threw his chicken back into the bucket, and stormed off.

Where the heck did that come from?

Aidan

My father loved his bourbon.

Hell, *I* loved his bourbon.

My feet were propped on his desk, the bottle he kept hidden away on his bookshelf hung loosely in my hands. I lost track of how much I drank. My head felt fuzzy. I almost forgot what upset me so much.

But Briana was a hard woman to forget. I had a picture of her up on my phone, propped against the monitor on the desk. Occasionally, I pressed a button to keep the phone from going to sleep so I could continue looking at her. For the life of me I couldn't figure out why she would leave so fast. No luck with Nikki when I asked her where Briana went, and even less with her aunt. Lora refused to speak to me and threatened to call the cops if I kept *"harassing"* her. Fuck that noise.

The entire conversation was too hard to relive, so I gave up.

One hell of a way spend the rest of my day.

I could barely eat. Mom went all out for our dinner, with fresh steaks from the farmer's market and organic mashed potatoes. Hell, she made so much food I couldn't remember everything she put on the table when we sat down to eat. She recently got into a major all-organic food kick. Though, now that I thought about it, Mom never claimed to be the type of woman to make anything from a box. She spent hours slaving in the kitchen and I almost felt bad because I holed myself in my father's study to drink myself to oblivion when I should've been out there enjoying time with my family.

"That's a three hundred dollar bottle of Evan Williams I wanted to save there, son."

I sank lower into Dad's chair and took another swig of the whiskey, just to prove how little I cared.

"I think I fucked up," I said.

Dad heaved a breath, sitting next to the same shelf where he kept his bourbon.

"How?"

"Briana."

"Cynthia's roommate?"

"Yeah. I fucked up. Don't know why. Don't know how. I think Mom and Cyn know something but they ain't telling me."

"Women keep secrets. I stopped trying to figure them out a long time ago."

"How the hell have you and Mom stayed married for so long?"

Dad released a sigh again. "I honestly can't say, son."

"You're no help. You know what? You're a sucky father."

Dad clunked his heavy boots on the wooden floor and snatched the bottle from my hands.

"The hell you do that for!?"

"I'm not a lousy father."

I snorted and pressed the button on my phone to keep Bri's picture up again.

"If you keep drinking at this rate, you'll kill yourself. It's been going on too long, son."

"I'm not drinking much..."

Things got fuzzier but the minute.

"Abs is gonna kill me, but you're going with me to your Grandma's for Thanksgiving."

I still can't remember anything after that.

I had one of my arms slung across my forehead when I took in a deep breath. My mouth instantly watered at the smell of bacon cooking. A rooster crowed so loud he sounded like he was right next to my head. I moved my arm, groaning because of the crick in my neck, and cracked open an eye.

It was still dark.

Who the hell was cooking?

This wasn't my mother's couch. Or my couch. Hell, it wasn't Cyn's futon for that matter either.

I didn't remember lying down to take a nap.

The rooster crowed a second, third, and fourth time. I pressed my eyes shut, grabbed the pillow under my head, and held it to my ears. It muffled the sound but it didn't shut out the bird. Maybe if he didn't shut up, chicken would be on the menu for dinner.

The soft *thing* moved underneath me and I buried my head into whatever it was.

"Get up, you lazy drunk!"

Bang! Bang! Bang!

Like a rocket, I shot up and rammed my head my former pillow's ass. The dog yelped and scampered away from me as fast as it could. When the hell did I get to my grandmother's house? She lived all the way in fucking North Carolina. Her poodle hid behind her.

"Shit, woman, quit banging those pots!" My grandfather growled as he walked past us.

"Son of a bitch..." I moaned, lying back down. The hangover hit me full force. "Grandma, knock it off."

She stopped banging the pots only to put her hand on her hip.

"I heard you're being a lush cause some girl broke your heart. That ain't no reason to be a fool and turn to the bottle," Grandma said.

"Where the hell is Dad?" I asked.

"You watch your mouth, boy," Grandma said.

"Rosie, why don't you leave Aidan alone and come help me in the kitchen?" said my Aunt Julia.

Christ, was *everyone* at my grandmother's?

I couldn't say her full house surprised me. My grandmother's house usually stayed full. Dad had three brothers and one of them recently married. Julia married Dad's youngest brother, Casey. I didn't know her well but she always seemed sweet whenever I spoke to her. My head throbbed like hell but I didn't miss her protruding belly poking out of the kitchen arch as she shook a spatula at my grandmother.

"*Rosie*! I need *that* skillet! Aidan, why don't you come in here for some aspirin and coffee, sweetie?"

"You still ain't up, boy?"

"What the hell are we doing in North Carolina for, Dad?"

"Your mother started bitchin'."

I closed my eyes for a minute, trying to make sense of what was going on. "What do you mean?"

"You know how she gets. She starts complaining when I do shit she doesn't agree with. She's not too excited about your drinking binge or how that Lora bitch treated you. She ain't too happy about us skipping out on the church Thanksgiving today, either."

"Oh, fuck," I said, groaning. I couldn't remember a damn thing past getting pissed off because Lora threatened to call the police on me if I showed up on her doorstep again. My head pounded. "How much did I drink?"

"You owe me money for my bourbon," Dad growled, walking past my grandmother.

"How the hell did I stay out for so long?"

I can't tell you off the top of my head how far it is from Tennessee to North Carolina, but I know it had to be a while.

"I ought to kick your father's ass," Grandma growled. "What the hell got into you? Takin' your boy drinking for a whole weekend?"

I sat up too fast. My head pounded but I forced myself to ignore it.

"*What?*" I asked. "We went drinking for two days straight?"

"I think we both needed it, son."

Dad almost looked worried about me but that's most I would get out of him on the matter. He shrugged and walked into the kitchen. "Hey Rosie, what you have cookin'?"

"Son of a bitch..." I moaned, pushing myself to my feet.

Damn.

My head *pounded*.

It was too early in the morning to think. If Dad thought Mom's level of bitching was bad before he took off with me—I still couldn't believe I didn't remember this—then he was in for a whole *new* level of getting bitched at when he finally decided to go home. I knew from experience that if Dad took off to his mother's, he would stay here for a while. A few times he tried to get Mom to sell the ranch to move to North Carolina—she could do her "horse thing" out here, in his words—but Mom refused. Dad missed his brothers so that's why I knew he liked it out here. In the summer he loved to go on fishing trips with Uncle Casey and Uncle Floyd.

"You coming to eat?" Uncle Floyd said, poking his head out of the kitchen.

"I think food is the last thing my stomach can handle right now," I said. "I think I need some more rest."

Grandma, furious, stormed off when Julia called for her again. I couldn't blame her for being angry at Dad. Hell, I wouldn't be surprised if Mom already knew exactly what happened and called and bitched at Grandma. That's why I got woken up with fucking pans scaring me the fuck awake.

I had no idea where the hell my phone was.

My grandmother insisted I keep a room in her large house even though I rarely saw her, so that's where I headed. I needed to know if I had my phone with me. Sure enough, Dad took enough time to pack some extra clothes. I dug around in the bag, wishing he at least thought to throw my stuff into a proper suitcase since he dragged me all the way out here. I dumped the whole bag onto the bed.

I stopped when I saw my phone. For a few moments I worried Dad forgot to grab it for me. It's a wonder I didn't lose it in my drinking binge. I turned it on and it beeped like crazy when the signal finally registered. Most of my missed calls were from Mom, but I also had a load of text messages from Cyn and Lee.

Lee: Where are you?
Cyn: What is up with you? You never acted so weird over a girl before. I swear nothing strange happened before she left. You're being ridiculous.

Lee: Dude, your mother is pissed. You should call us. I'm rehoming Daisy so you can quit being sore at me.
Cyn: Aidan! What the hell is going on? Nikki told Lee that Lora threatened to call the cops on you or something? You need to let me know what's up.

    I didn't read the rest of the messages. They were all comprised of the same thing, though as I glanced at them, I did see something from Cynthia asking if we would be okay now that we broke up. I didn't know how to answer her, figuring I would take care of it when I got home. She knew our relationship ended because things wouldn't work out with the two of us. We fell in love with different people because we grew apart. I accepted that the moment I realized I loved Bri. I might not have been sure where she was currently, but I knew I loved her. Whatever was going on, she would get back in contact with me. I had to believe it.
    The temptation to drink again roared up but I felt like I had a white-hot poker searing my brain, so I decided against it. I smelled breakfast in the kitchen and my stomach turned, whether from being sick or hungry I couldn't decide. Touching the poisonous shit Dad liked to drink was off limits from now on. I'd stick to beer, something my grandfather always had plenty of in the fridge.
    For the life of me, I couldn't figure out why Briana would move back to Kentucky. Her brother got in trouble for drugs up there. Didn't she worry that might happen again?
    Well, Kevin smoked pot. I felt bad for the kid. Bri was a great girl but she let herself get stressed out too fast and too often about her brother and Lora.

I hated the bitch.

Seriously, who threatens to call the cops on a concerned boyfriend? Well, we weren't official, but that didn't mean I didn't care. I needed to figure out what happened; if I did something wrong. How would I know how I fucked up if I couldn't talk to Briana? She had to know I'd be willing to fix whatever it was that I screwed up on. *Had to*, but Lora wouldn't tell me a fucking thing.

I sucked in a deep breath and told myself not to be an asshole.

It wasn't anyone's fault. Briana was her own person. She would call me if she needed me. I let out another deep breath, and stood. I found a plug near the lamp next to the bed and plugged in my phone.

"Hey sweetie."

My aunt leaned against the doorjamb. She rested one hand against her pregnant belly, a tray with a plate and glass in the other while she looked at me. I understood why people said pregnant women glowed. She smiled at me wide, her long black hair touching her stomach in a braid.

"Hey, Julia," I said.

"Are you thinking about your girl again?"

I cleared my throat, closed out the text messages, and set my phone down. I scrubbed my face again then shook my head.

"No," I said. "Why?"

"Aidan, it's written all over your face, honey. She's all you could talk about when your Daddy dragged you in the house drunk as a skunk." She somewhat waddled while she walked over to me. "Here, I figured you wouldn't want to hear more of

Rosie's complaining about the way you and your father showed up."

I saw the medicine next to the glass of orange juice. I gratefully grabbed that first and swallowed down the pills.

"Come on, Aidan," Julia sighed. "I know that's why you drank."

"No offense, but you haven't known my family long, Julia," I said. "Maybe random drinking and road trips are normal for me and my father."

Julia raised an eyebrow. "You do realize me and Casey dated longer than we've been married, right? I was under the impression you that aren't close to your Dad because this is the first time I've *ever* seen you up."

I clenched my jaw and realized I acting like a dick.

"Yeah. I miss Briana."

"Well..." Julia said. "I realize we don't know each other well, but why don't you tell me what happened, anyway?"

Casey ran past the bedroom door, a hand over his mouth. I heard another door slam open and shut followed by a load of retching. Disgusted, I pushed my orange juice away.

I took in a deep breath. Talking about her wasn't something I liked to do lately.

"I... for a while, she was my ex-girlfriend's roommate. That's how we met."

I ended up telling her everything. I told her how we worked with Blue Moon to get him comfortable with ropes. Well, how *Briana* worked with him. How Cynthia kept pushing the two of us to date. How I slowly fell in love with her... still loved her.

My headache was worse by the end of it, but at least I vented to get it off my chest.

Julia sighed.

"That's a hell of a story."

I decided I was hungry so I took another bite of eggs. They were colder but I ate them anyway.

"Well, I can't figure out why she left," I said.

"Do you think Cynthia said anything to upset her after the two of you broke up?"

"Nah, Cyn wouldn't do that. She's been just as worried about Briana as me. Bri's friend won't tell us anything and her aunt is..." I sighed. "I figure I better to leave her alone."

Julia smiled at me and placed her hand over mine. "Have you ever heard the saying, 'If you love something, let it go. If it comes back to you, it's yours forever, but if it doesn't it wasn't ever meant to be'?"

"That sounds like something Bri would say," I said.

I reached for my phone. My fingers itched to look through my last text messages to her again. I couldn't figure out what happened. Had I sounded too clingy? Too desperate to find out why she left? Had I scared her off when I admitted I was in love with her in front of my ex-girlfriend and mother? I kept analyzing it but couldn't figure it out.

"Well, I think whatever is going on, she might come back to you," Julia said.

I scoffed. "You've never even met her. How can you be sure?"

Julia patted my hand and winked. "I swear this baby has given me the gift of premonitions. The other day I knew it when my best friend met a new guy."

I snorted in laughter at her.

"All joking aside, if this girl cared about you? She won't be able to stay away from you for long. I think you need to give whatever happened some time and she'll contact you eventually."

"It's been since like November seventeenth," I said. "I don't think she wants to get a hold of me. She changed her phone number."

"Yeah, but you're online like everyone else right? Has she blocked anything like email, Facebook, Twitter?"

I snorted. "I don't care much for the social media crap. Cynthia always uses it. I have more important shit to do than be on a computer."

"Yeah, but you could try messaging her if she's online. Or email her. Let her know you miss her and you don't understand what happened. It's not hard to find someone's address either, Aidan."

"I don't want to come off a stalker," I said.

Julia patted my hand again and then stood up. "You can keep telling yourself she'll think of you that way if you want to but something tells me she won't, honey."

"I just think that if she could leave so fast, then maybe I need to leave her alone," I said.

"That's your business, but did you ever think you might be making a mistake by letting her get away so easy? You don't have to go through her friend or aunt to find her. And don't blame my hormones for my incredibly silly suggestions."

I frowned at her.

Julia rolled her eyes. "Come on, you know that's what you were about to say to me."

I clenched my jaw, not sure what to say.

A loud retch from the bathroom filled the hallway. Julia rolled her eyes. "I better go check on Casey...then kick his ass for drinking so much."

I realized somewhere in that chat with her I was mostly okay. My stomach felt tender but my hangover wasn't as bad as I thought it was. I swallowed down another drink of orange juice but was sure I'd keep everything down. The headache had dulled down to a throb behind my eyes.

"Hey," I said when she started to leave the room.

Julia peeked her head back into the door. "Yeah?"

"Thanks," I said. "I think I needed to talk."

Julia smiled wide. "Any time. It's been fun meeting you, Aidan. I'm glad I could take on my duties as your aunt seriously."

I laughed when she left the room, not saying another word. Uncle Casey married an interesting woman, that's for sure, and I couldn't help but shake my head at her.

I sighed, and looked at my phone again. I knew I should have at least called Mom back, but decided against it. They could all wait to hear from me. Dad was right in bringing me to my grandmother's.

Briana

I clenched my fists together on Evie's porch, shaking in anger.

"I'm moving back to Kentucky!"

I couldn't believe Lora drove all the way just to come get us barely four days after Thanksgiving. Kevin was supposed to start school back since it was a Monday and Lora was supposed to be at work. Instead, here she was, demanding we come back home even though I called the school to ask them what I would have to do to make sure I could get everything squared away to transfer him to another high school.

"The hell you aren't coming back," Lora said.

"There's *nothing* in Tennessee for me."

Even saying the name of the state felt bitter on my tongue. I had nothing there that would benefit me in any way. It would be a waste of gas to go back there to pick up my stuff. That's why I wanted Lora to get my things from Cynthia's apartment. Running into Aidan would be unavoidable so I didn't want to risk going back. We no longer had a home in Tennessee. I'd already withdrawn from my classes at Shiloh University.

The plan had been to have Lora come up here with my stuff on a weekend, when she wouldn't need to worry about missing work. Kevin told me he didn't want to change schools so close to the semester being over, but I didn't even plan on giving him a choice. I wanted to move somewhere like Winchester or Richmond, where he wouldn't be around the same kids he was around when we lived here. He would be fine as long as he didn't go to his old school. Maybe I should have transferred him somewhere else rather than moving us to an entirely different state in the first place.

I recently finished arguing with him about going back to Tennessee when Lora knocked on the door.

I was... I was done; with Aidan, with Cynthia, even with Nikki.

"You're going to give up your entire education because you're stupid and forgot to use a condom?"

"Lora!"

"All right," Evie said, stepping behind me and opening the door wider. "I'm trying to eat my dinner. I don't need the two of you screaming at each other while I'm trying to enjoy it."

I stared blankly at Evie. I almost hoped she would help me considering that she told me to do what I thought was right for myself.

"But—"

"I think you aren't making good decisions right now," Evie said. "Sorry kid. You're not. You need to figure out how you're going to handle things on your own and you won't do it unless we show you some tough love."

"This is ridiculous!" I screeched.

Lora huffed when Evie slammed her door. "*Answer me*, young lady. Do you expect me to let you give up your entire education so you can move back up here, and what? Raise a *baby*?"

"Yeah," I said, turning to her. "I think that's what I'm doing. I'm moving back to Kentucky with my brother so I can raise my baby and let them both grow up here."

"If you do, I'm challenging your ability to take care of Kevin. I should have taken custody of him when your parents died. I think I might go after your baby, too, if you move back to Kentucky."

My cheeks flushed in sudden anger.

"Like *hell* you will!" I said. "You're way out of line!"

"I'm not trying to judge you, sweetie. I'm worried about you. You can't move every time life gets hard."

"I love how you can threaten to take my unborn baby and my brother, then tell me you're worried about me," I almost growled. "Besides, who says I can't move?"

That's the most childish reaction I had during my whole my situation so far. I was exhausted.

"You're going to do this to yourself? Briana, I get that you decided to drop out of college, but your brother is actually doing well in the high school *we* decided he needed to go to because of the issues he had before you moved. You keep telling me you want to approach life like an adult. You aren't right now."

I hated admitting it when Lora was right.

"If I come back, everyone will find out," I said, hugging myself. "I don't want anyone to know I'm pregnant. Hell, Nikki thinks I moved."

Lora brushed back her auburn hair and shoved her keys into her jeans. "I think you need a break from all of those people, baby girl. So much for going to college to study, huh?"

That did it. Tears ran down my face and I laugh-sobbed then nodded.

"Fine! I'll come home! Stop threatening to take my baby and my brother away from me."

Lora sighed then pulled me into a hug. "I wish you gave me another way to convince you to come home. I *hate* being the bad guy."

Chapter Three

Aidan

"Son of a bitch!"

Dad slammed his fist on the front door. We got back from a long drive from North Carolina only to find out Mom changed the locks on us.

I *couldn't* blame Mom. No matter how many times I told him we had to go home, Dad insisted on staying with his mother. He kept us there until the fucking week before Christmas. I could have gotten us home sooner but he didn't grab my wallet before he decided to take me on his unplanned trip to see his family.

I still shudder every time I hear what Mom yelled at Dad through the phone.

"What the hell is wrong with you? Aidan is hurting right now because he doesn't know where Briana is and you drag him off for a drinking binge! I had no idea where you were for weeks! I ought to divorce your ass! And Lee! That boy has his head shoved so far up Cynthia's ass there isn't any use in trying to talk some sense into him!"

"I can't believe she changed the locks on me," Dad growled out.

"You should've known taking off to Grandma's would piss her off."

"If the wind hits that woman's neck the wrong way she gets pissed off," Dad said, kicking the front door.

"Whoa," I said, making him take a step back. "The last thing we need to do is to break the door. Mom will only get angrier."

"I hate it when she does this shit," Dad said. "She does it every time I go see my parents."

It was difficult to count on both my hands how many times Mom became angry and Dad for changed the locks on him. Trips to his mother's lasting for weeks weren't uncommon, though, so I wasn't actually worried they would get a divorce. Mom loved to throw empty threats at him in order to try to get her way whenever she became furious with him. I can't deny that seeing family in North Carolina wasn't a bad thing though. I'd needed it, and I hadn't even realized it until we were already there.

"Don't ever get married," Dad said. "You might be aching and missing that Briana girl right now but you're better off, kid."

Dad glared at the front door like it offended him. Laughing, I clapped Dad on the back then pulled my phone out, not sure what to say to him.

I was sure I'd end up married, not that I counted my chickens before they hatched. I wanted marriage, even if it wouldn't be Briana. I could hope for miracles though, right? It was useless to think that would ever happen; foolish to give myself false hope. I thought about the past few days while I was with family, watching Casey and Julia together. I wanted that. I craved it. I needed to get my mind off Briana. To do that, maybe I needed to start dating again. No, I wasn't ready yet. Maybe eventually, but for once I needed to enjoy being single. Just because Briana decided to disappear on me didn't mean I needed to jump into something new right way. Something told me that would be a mistake.

I don't know why the hell I worried about it so much. Cynthia mentioned something about it being time for me to move on from Bri's in text message about moving. I didn't respond to it because I didn't want to encourage her to find me a date. Everything with Briana still felt too fresh. "Come on," I said. "We're both tired. You can crash at my place."

"I shouldn't have to fucking crash at your place," Dad growled even though he followed me back to the car.

"The two of you can get your shit sorted out later," I said to him. "Right now I'm just tired as hell."

Briana

"I think you need to give the baby up for adoption."

I stared blankly at Lora. Kevin glanced between the two of us, blew out a sharp breath, and pulled his music player out of his hoodie. He shoved his ear buds in and turned the music up so loud I heard it across the kitchen table. It was his prerogative if he wanted to ruin his ear drums, so I said nothing to him. I couldn't blame him for not wanting to hear me or Lora fight over her constant attempt to tell me what to do about my baby.

"I'm not giving my kid up for adoption," I said, standing. I needed to do something. I couldn't sit there and let her stare at me, acting so *judgmental*. "I thought we were done talking about this until after the holidays."

We stared each other down. Kevin loudly grabbed the box of sugar cookies sitting on the table between me and Lora. She tapped her nails on the wood in agitation.

Lora rolled her eyes. "So you're giving your life up? You're twenty-one, Briana. You're so close to having your bachelor's degree."

I needed something to do. Something to drink. I grabbed a glass and turned toward the sink, turning on the tap. The water served as a fresh, cool reminder that even though things felt out of control, they really weren't. I stopped gulping down the water for a second, reminding myself to breathe. Breathing was a good thing. I needed to calm down, and to go easy on the water. I didn't want to run to the bathroom every five minutes on Christmas Day.

Lora wasn't acting judgmental; she cared for me. Kevin also caught her spiking her rum with eggnog.

No, *really*. She used a little eggnog for her rum.

"You don't even need a closed adoption," Lora said. "It can be open. The adoptive parents can send you pictures and you can keep in touch with them. It doesn't mean you'll never see your kid again. You'll be able to live your life and you can start a family when you're ready."

I slammed my glass of water onto the kitchen table so hard it splashed everywhere.

"Shit, Briana!" Kevin said.

"Watch your mouth!" I said.

"*Hey*," Lora said. "You do not get to act that way then yell at your brother!"

"I'm his guardian!"

"You're still living under my rules, in my house, while you get things figured out until you have the baby.

"Lora, I love you, but I'm twenty-one. I'm not a kid anymore. I'm perfectly capable of raising a baby and Kevin."

"You may be capable, but you're not mature enough to be a mother. You *barely* take care of Kevin."

"I'm abandoning ship while the two of you fight this out," Kevin grabbed his bowl of cereal and shoving his music player into his pocket. "Please don't kill each other. I don't want to clean my aunt or my sister's blood off the walls when we should be watching Rudolph movies and eating candy canes."

I narrowed my eyes at him. "Very funny."

"Try putting your claws away and having a conversation without them," Kevin suggested with a wide grin. I huffed at him when he pulled me into a side-hug and let him kiss me on the cheek. I didn't blame my brother for bailing. Lora and I were slowly reaching a boiling point in her opinions on what I should do when I had the baby and all three of us knew it. It wasn't enough. I decided to come back so Kevin could finish out the year. Lora wasn't satisfied with just being worried about me since I was pregnant. She pushed and pushed and pushed until I wanted to scream at her.

"Don't you dare turn your PlayStation on," Lora said. "I'm having a *Bones* marathon on Netflix after I get done having a conversation with your sister."

"You," I said, pointing to my aunt. "A *Bones* marathon? Seriously? And I'm not the immature one? It's *Christmas*, for God's sake. Let's do normal family Christmassy stuff! If Kev wants to play video games later, he can play them! What is the use in getting him three new games if we don't let him?"

"It's unhealthy for him to play games all day!"

"He's a *teenager!*" I scoffed. "He can eat us out of the house and not gain an inch! God, you're barely in your thirties and you're acting younger than me! How am *I* the immature one?"

"I don't think you're capable of ever being successful if you have a child right now," Lora said. "You got into a relationship with a guy who already had a girlfriend and it's because you weren't responsible that you ended up pregnant. You can't even *let* him know about your situation. What are you going to do if you keep the baby? Get Aidan to pay child support? Keep the fact that he's got a child from him for the rest of his life? No, Briana, you're *not* ready for a baby."

"I thought you wanted to help me. That's what I'm taking; *your help*. I thought we were family. I thought I could rely on you but instead I just keep hearing the same old thing and I'm getting *sick* of it!"

Lora stomped to the refrigerator. If I hadn't been so pissed I might have stopped to laugh at her red face and unbrushed hair.

"I told you—*told you*—you needed to be careful. You needed to study. You promised me. I want you to have a life, Briana."

"Oh," I said, laughing.

"Infants need a lot of care. They poop, they cry, and they can't even hold their heads up."

It was impossible to think Lora was the aunt who, a while ago, decided it would be fun to leave my brother alone and go party with her friends.

I almost, *almost,* forgot about it, too.

"You could barely keep your brother out of trouble when you lived in Kentucky. I'm afraid to think what will happen now that you're pregnant and still won't tell Aidan about it."

"I'm sorry, I thought he wasn't allowed on your property!"

Lora froze mid-step toward the stove.
"What?"

"Oh, yeah," I said. "I heard about that. Screaming at him at the top of your lungs for him to get off your property and threatening to call the cops for harassing you. You're going to call the cops on Aidan, really? If he shows up again?"

Lora spun around to look at me again. "Yeah, I wanted to call the cops on him. I was angry over how you got yourself into this situation and he wouldn't stop trying to get me to tell him where you were."

My heart did something funny. It skipped a beat, or something, and I felt nausea burning at the pit of my stomach, so I took a seat. I wasn't sure why I couldn't tell him about the pregnancy yet. I wasn't ready. I'd barely accepted I was pregnant.

I took in a deep breath.

"I'm not sure if it will again," Lora said. "Will it? Are you going to keep hiding from him? Hell, you're hiding from your best friend right now. I can't even tell you how many times I've dodged telling Nikki where you are because you forbade me from uttering a word."

"I need time to myself right now," I said. "I think that's not something unreasonable to ask for."

"I just think you shouldn't write off giving the baby up for adoption. You don't want to get rid of it—I think it's too late for that now."

The way Cyn looked so sad when she told me she had an abortion almost a year ago flashed through my mind. I shook my head venomously and glared at Lora for even mentioning anything that would end up in me hurting the baby. I didn't care what she said. I had life growing inside of me. Abortion might be an option for a woman who truly didn't want to give birth, who truly wasn't ready to be a mother yet, but I felt like I would be acting selfish if I did it when I was perfectly capable of being a mom. I hadn't managed to totally screw my brother up yet. I knew, realistically, that it would be different because I would have an infant. There were new challenges there I hadn't needed to face when my brother was born because my parents were there to raise him and I was a little kid at the time anyway.

I stood back up, pushed my water away, and started to leave the kitchen.

"Our conversation isn't done yet, Briana. Sit back down."

I spun around. "I'll stop walking away when you stop being mean and hypocritical. And you're drunk. Don't think we didn't notice you covering rum up with egg nog."

We stared at each other some more. That's all. Just stared, saying nothing. I knew exactly what went through her mind, though. She wasn't the best role model for my brother, but at least he had been safe.

I had to wonder, though, if I really was making a mistake.

I needed to be alone in my room. Lora didn't stop me. At least she realized I needed to be alone for a while. I felt too stressed out and suddenly nauseous to stay in there to try for any kind of civil conversation with her. Kevin waved at me on the way to my bedroom and I waved back, but we said not a word to each other. He seemed concerned, but we would talk later when I was ready.

Aidan had a right to know he would be a father soon, right? That I was pregnant? I woke up every morning and told myself he needed to know. I felt silly for changing my phone number. I wasn't even sure why I hid from Nikki.

I didn't want to throw up. I hated this part of the morning, and even worse, it was harder to fight back whenever Lora upset me. I laid on my bed and sucked in a few deep breaths of air even while my mouth watered and I fisted my hands into my blankets so I wouldn't lose the water I drank moments before.

No. Know what? Screw it. He could wait to find out I got pregnant, if I ever decided to tell him.

"Bri..." Lora asked, knocking lightly on my door before she poked her head inside a few minutes later. "Are you okay?"

I shook my head no and covered my hand with my mouth. She frowned at me.

"Bri... honey, are you okay?" Lora repeated.

I shook my head no before I sucked in a deep breath.

"What is that god awful smell?" I managed to choke.

Lora had a plate in her hands.

"Huh? Oh. I didn't want to get you sick so I thought you might want a peanut butter sandwich." Lora looked down at the plate. "I have a turkey in the oven. You know... since we're trying to be a normal family today... That's another reason you shouldn't raise this baby. You keep forgetting to eat right!"

Turkey?

Yep.

Right there.

Normally I loved poultry, but I gagged and made a beeline for the bathroom. No Christmas turkey for me.

I stared at myself in the mirror a few minutes later. I hadn't had a shower or brushed my hair yet so a lot of flyaway hair escaped my elastic. Since I got pregnant, my skin started to break out like I was a teenager all over again. I had a giant zit forming on the corner of my chin.

When had I started crying? Lora seemed determined to think Aidan wouldn't want me to have the baby since Cynthia had an abortion. I tried not to think about it too often.

I *wanted* to tell the truth to Aidan but I honestly needed a break from everyone who I could possibly avoid.

I sniffed, shook my head, and couldn't believe how scattered my thoughts were. Nikki was the closest thing to a sister to me but I hadn't talked to her since sometime before Thanksgiving. I don't think I'd done that since we were thirteen when we got into a silly argument over something I can't remember anymore.

The knock on the door startled me.

"Are you okay, Bri?" Kevin knocked again. "Lora wanted me to check on you before the bus gets here!"

"Yeah, Kev, I'm fine!"

My voice broke. I wiped the tears out of my eyes. I didn't want my brother to see me crying. Even though I tried to hide it from him, I didn't do the best job.

"Somehow, I don't believe you."

He came inside. I kept trying to figure out when my baby brother started growing into a man. He still had a long way to go, but I noticed changes in him that hadn't been there before we moved to Tennessee. He took out the trash without Lora asking, constantly checked on me as he did now, and did his homework without us asking him to.

"You're not okay," Kevin said.

I refused to make eye contact with him. Instead I stared at my toothbrush and wiped my eyes. I regretted not locking the bathroom door.

I couldn't let him see me break down. I was the older sibling. I was supposed to have all the answers after our parents died.

"I'm fine," I said, sucking in a deep breath. I turned around to face him and crossed my arms over my chest. "Morning sickness just sucks."

"Everything is making you sick." Kevin wrapped his earbuds around his music player and shoved it into his hoodie. "What's wrong, sis? You still freaking out because Lora wants you to give the baby up for adoption?"

I sucked in another sharp breath before I could stop myself.

Lora knew abortion wasn't an option. I couldn't do it. It wasn't the baby's fault that I was an idiot who slept with such a complicated guy, and that we forgot to use protection. I thought I wanted the baby too, at first. Kevin tried to tell me he would help any way he could, but I couldn't ask my brother to help me raise my kid. I'd never reach goals in life if I became a mom—or that's what Lora told me. She could stick her opinions about single parents where the sun won't shine. It was kind of hard to like her right now because she lectured me every chance she got. I was almost thankful for the nausea and an excuse to run from her because I'm sure the talk about adoption would have happened again.

I understood why she suggested it, though. She wanted me to finish school. She wanted me to have a life. She didn't like Aidan very much because of how our relationship started. I hadn't told her, though, that he'd broken up with Cynthia before I fell off Blue Moon, although I gathered Nikki probably told her that already.

I burst into sobs.

"Crap, Briana."

I tried to fight it when Kevin wrapped his arms around me but eventually I just gave in. Kevin sighed and squeezed me tight.

"You know Lora is just trying to look out for you, right? I don't have any doubt you can raise this baby. I'm not too happy with Aidan, but you really need to do what is right for you and stop listening to everyone for once."

I pulled back and wiped my eyes. "That's just the thing. I'm about to become a mother. I don't come first anymore."

"Bullshit."

"You *really* need to watch your language."

We released each other from the hug.

"I'm fifteen now," Kevin said. "I think I should be able to swear."

I frowned at him, done crying, and crossed my arms. "I don't care. You shouldn't be using that language. If you do again, I'll make you do what Mom used to make me do."

Kevin widened his eyes in exaggeration, something he always liked to do out of sarcasm. "Oh no, not *sentences!*"

"Oh, I will," I threatened, trying my hardest to continue acting stern when all I really wanted to do was laugh at him. "A thousand of them."

We stared at each other for a minute before we both burst into laughter. I needed this. I needed my brother, so he could be there for me, and my aunt, so she could be hard on me even though she made me so mad.

"I don't get why Lora is so worried," Kevin said. "You've got this parenting thing down."

Aidan

Mom didn't like to open presents on Christmas until after dinner. The whole night Lee fidgeted and couldn't keep his eyes off of Cynthia. Her mother, Beth, and grandmother, Sharon, were there. I couldn't help but feel awkward as hell because Sharon kept glaring at me like I'd done something wrong to her sweet, sweet granddaughter.

Cynthia and I knew both it was a load of bullshit.

She still ate up the attention. I told Mom she shouldn't invite Sharon and Beth, but she wouldn't listen, and said if Cynthia was going to be here on Christmas Day, then so should her family.

It didn't help watching Cyn cozy up to Lee the entire night.

It wasn't that I wanted to be with her again. Hell no. I just missed being in a relationship. Seeing the two of them act so loving with each other had me thinking about Briana nonstop and it drove me crazy. I hoped her day went well. I wanted nothing more than to talk to her; maybe beg Nikki to help me get in contact with her, but recently I heard Briana completely shut her best friend out too. I tried to get Mom and Cyn to tell me what happened after she fell off the horse but the two of them refused to talk to me, their jaws clenched than snapping turtle.

"What is going on with them tonight?" I asked Mom, staring at my cousin and ex-girlfriend, trying to figure out why he was acting more affectionate toward Cyn.

Was it just because her mother and grandmother were here? Or was it for another reason, like that he was acting overly gracious because Sharon fell in love with his dog and decided to take her for him?

"I'm not sure," Mom said, crossing her arms. "He is up Cyn's ass tonight, isn't he? Sharon and Beth are even more prudish and up themselves than I remember them being."

"*Mom*," I said.

"What?" she asked, a façade of innocence written all over her face while she sliced into the ham. "I don't play well with other women."

I rolled my eyes. Mom acted like the epitome of a perfect hostess while Dad joked with me and Lee and took out some of his Evan Williams for us to take a couple shots.

"You shouldn't let Dad drag out the bourbon."

Mom rolled her eyes. "Those women are so boring," she said, leaning in closer to whisper, "I needed to take a few shots to put up with them too! Don't even get me started on your father. I'm still so angry with him for taking off like he did for Thanksgiving. I have half a mind to dump the rest of his bourbon over his head and lock him out of the bedroom for a night."

Dad shifted uncomfortably but said nothing. He'd been in hot water with Mom since we got back.

I couldn't help it. I burst into laughter.

"You dodged a bullet there, I'd hate to have that woman as an in-law," Mom said.

"Will you quit? I forgot how mean you get when you drink," I said, chuckling.

Mom slid a piece of ham into her mouth. "You don't know what you're talking about, son."

Lee cleared his throat loud enough for us to hear him. He stood, pushing the dining room chair back, and took Cynthia's hand. She stared at him, eyes wide.

"So, I was going to wait to do this until later, but I can't wait anymore."

What the hell got into him? I glanced at Mom, hoping she might have the answer, but she didn't seem like she knew what was going on any more than I did. Dad grinned, however, and relaxed in his chair. Beth gasped, her hand flying to her mouth. Sharon scowled.

"Cynthia, I know we haven't been together very long, but you mean the world to me, baby. We might not have gotten together under the best circumstances, but I feel like you're *it* for me. We can't do anything else but move forward." His voice broke, choking a bit, as he reached into his jeans and pulled something out.

An engagement ring.

"Marry me, Cyn."

My fucking cousin proposed to my ex.

I couldn't take it anymore. I was happy for them and all that shit, but I merely grabbed Dad's bottle of bourbon and headed in the direction of his study. Watching that hurt too fucking much.

A few days later, I watched my herd graze next to a broken fence and pulled my hood over my head. Shaking, I shoved my hands into my pockets. I needed to add supplies to fix the fence to my list of shit I needed to do that day.

January weather sucked. Always did. Then again I preferred summer over any other season, when I could ditch long sleeves.

Epona and another foal perked up their ears, staring at me for a second before they bolted in another direction. Faith watched over at Epona for a moment, swished her tail, and then resumed grazing. Blue Moon flicked his tail too and inched closer to sniff her but she reared her ears back and nipped him.

I shook my head, laughing. I couldn't leave my horse alone outside for nothing. Not only had Blue Moon destroyed the fence keeping him and a couple other horses separated from each other, he'd obviously shown Faith his favorite grazing spot underneath a burr bush.

Without Bri—no, I wouldn't think about her.

She made herself clear. She moved. Had her friend pack up her stuff, and changed her number. I needed to try to move on, too.

I drew in a deep breath and opened the gate. "What the hell did you go and break the fence for?"

Blue Moon's head shot up, both ears lied flat. He eyed the lead rope but let me hook it to his halter anyway, grabbing for my hair.

"Shit," I hissed, tapping his nose. I pulled my ponytail from his teeth but Blue Moon was pissed off at me so he snorted loudly and made to bite at me again. I stepped away quickly and jerked down on the lead rope.

I deserved that. I had Cyn and Lee on a strict order not to let him have any sugar cubes because Briana spoiled him on them. Now he was pissed and determined to nip anything he could to find the damn things. I shook my head at myself, frustrated because I couldn't stop thinking about her that day for some reason. I was determined not to miss her but I did anyway. It started to piss me off.

Blue Moon pushed me forward with his nose, following me out of the gate and to the barn. If I was going to do this, I had to do it now.

"You're right," said Stanley Davis when we got inside the barn. His wife and my mother knitted together. They had a few horses but they mostly just kept them as pets for an occasional ride. "The girls will love him."

"He's a good horse. He's been on a few trail rides but has an issue with men."

To prove my point, Blue Moon pushed both of his ears back and tried to grab my ponytail again. I pushed him away and took a tighter hold of his halter.

"Loves women, though."

Stanley took a cautious step back. "Well, I don't see any problem with that. I'm sure I could get him to trust me. My daughter will think he's magnificent."

I hated that damn word in correlation to horses. Magnificent, like Blue Moon was some kind of trophy to be had. He was my buddy, but I just couldn't keep him anymore.

"Oh, yeah?" I asked. I pulled a carrot out of my pocket and shoved it into Blue's mouth. That would stop him for a few minutes. "How old is she?"

"She's twenty-one. I think your girlfriend is one of her friends, actually."

"Oh, if you're talking about Cyn, we broke up." I shrugged. "But he's a good horse in general to ride."

"Aidan—just what in hell do you think you're doing?"

I stood straighter and pushed my shoulders back at the sound of my mother's angry voice. Shit. I hoped I could cut a deal with Stanley before she even realized Blue was gone.

"Stan, you mind waiting back up at the house? I need to talk to my son about something."

"Well... I guess so. How much are you thinking for—?"

"This horse ain't for sale," Mom said. "None of them are in this field since most of them were rescues. Now, you want a Thoroughbred? We'll talk about that if you're interested."

Shit. This was worse than the time she found me and Lee drinking whiskey together down near the river when we were still kids. We got messed up that night. As soon as Mom found us, she dragged us back to the house by our ears. It was the worst fucking hangover I ever had in my entire life. She rounded on me as soon as Stanley left with a grunt, but agreed to talk to her about the Thoroughbreds later.

"Ow! Mom, what the hell?"

She pinched me. Actually pinched me on the shoulder.

"What's wrong with you?"

"Nothing!"

"What the hell are you trying to sell Blue for? You love him to death." She unhooked the lead rope from my horse, turned him around, and swatted his butt. He left, no further incentive needed.

"I just need him gone," I said. "We rescued him. He's trained. It's time to find him another home."

"You're mad at him because Briana left."

Shit.

Mom always saw right through me. I looked away from her. I couldn't stand the way she judged my decision to get rid of my horse. It was my decision. If I hadn't let Briana ride him that day maybe I would have never entertained the thought. There had been an accident. I had no idea where she was now.

"No I'm not," I tried anyway.

Mom threw her head back and laughed at me. "You are so much like your Daddy sometimes. Get caught doing something else and you automatically start acting like a scolded baby. We ain't selling Blue Moon. It's not his fault Briana left. It's enough I had to make Lee get rid of his dog because she was a nuisance to the horses!"

I sighed in defeat as Mom's words sank in.

"Damn," I said.

I needed to lean against something, to take a minute. My anger at my horse was misplaced and I knew that, but I decided to try to get rid of him anyway. It would break Briana's heart if I found him a home someplace else and she didn't know.

"I ought to skin you and your father's hides for staying gone for so long. You should've been hounding Nikki and Bri's aunt to tell you where she is, not running off to have a drinking fest with your father."

I sighed.

"Christ, Mom! It's not like we aren't grown men. We were visiting family."

"I had to spend so much time alone. It was awful," Mom said, her eyes watering. "Lee was all wrapped up in Cynthia and I'm just as worried about Briana as you are."

"She left. There's nothing I can do about it."

"You just don't want to try hard enough," Mom said.

I sighed. "You need to stop changing the locks on Dad whenever you get mad at him. It's not wrong for him to want to go see family."

"It is when he ups and leaves and takes my boy without any kind of explanation. I was worried sick 'til Rosie called. Why on earth did you all leave so suddenly?"

"We left because our boy scared me, Abs." Mom and I turned to look at Dad. "Found him drinking bourbon alone in my office. I didn't know what else to do so I took him with me. Sorry we scared you, baby."

Mom crossed her arms and glared at my father. I looked at her, really looked at her, and today she looked a little bit older. Her hair was piled on top of her head in a messy bun.

Shit. I'd been so wrapped up in my misery over Briana leaving, I hadn't been paying attention to my mother. Tears welled up in her eyes.

I sighed. "Come here, Mom."

I hugged her tight. Mom wouldn't sob. She wasn't much of a crier. But I could tell hearing that I'd been alone drinking in Dad's office got to her. Add that to the fact that we left her on the holidays?

"Come here, Abs," Dad said after a few minutes. "I'm sorry."

Mom shook her head, and I held her tighter. Dad sighed. They were officially in a fight. I hated it when my parents fought. It happened too much for my own liking, but I never knew how to make things better for them, so instead I just held Mom. She complained sometimes that she couldn't hold me like this sometimes since I wasn't a kid anymore.

"We're both assholes," I said.

Mom shook her head some more and pulled away from me. "No, don't say that. I know you're hurting because of what happened with Bri. Sweetie, selling Blue Moon isn't the answer."

She glared at Dad. He knew he was in deep shit, but at least maybe I'd be able to try to get Mom to change the locks back or give him a new key.

"You're right," I said. "I…"

I trailed off, not sure what to say.

"I think you're a big dumbass for not driving up to Kentucky to find her, but I can't say much on the matter," Mom said. "I'm just glad you're back. I can't stand how...involved—," Mom scrunched her nose up in disgust at the word. "Cyn and Lee keep disappearing when she's supposed to be working."

I sighed. Shit. I did not want to deal with my ex-girlfriend and cousin.

"I need to talk to them," I said.

Focusing on them would give me a chance to stop thinking about how I missed Bri so damn bad.

"Yeah, you do that," Mom said. "And tell Cynthia that if she doesn't start doing her job then I think she needs to stop coming to work."

"Now Mom, don't be that way."

"Well I'm getting sick and tired of having to grab her attention from Lee whenever she's here and she's supposed to be doing something with the horses. She's been worse than she was with you, not doing much work."

"She's busy dealing with her mom and grandmother before the new semester starts. Give her some slack, Mom. Her parents are going through a nasty divorce."

Mom crossed her arms and frowned.

"All right," I said, "I'll go and talk to them." I started to turn around, but then stopped.

"You're pissed off about a whole hell of a lot more than Cyn and Lee getting engaged, aren't you?"

Mom's lower lip spread thin and she sniffed.

"Involves me, doesn't it?"

Mom rolled her eyes and crossed her arms. "I don't know what you're talking about. Cyn just isn't doing her job and I'm getting tired of it."

"I might have to call bullshit."

"Call all the bullshit you want, I need to talk to a man about selling a horse now that you've got him interested in one. You track down Cyn and Lee. I need them to clean out the stables."

How could I not think Mom was hiding something from me?

I looked everywhere for Cyn and Lee but couldn't find them.

I didn't fucking understand women.

But I figured that since they weren't anywhere else to be found, that I might find them in Lee's bedroom.

I should have fucking knocked.

"Are you kidding me?"

Both of them, buck naked, with Cyn bent over Lee's dresser. Lee barely managed to grab a blanket before I slammed the door shut.

That was more than I ever wanted to see of my cousin's ass. Not that I hadn't seen Cyn naked before, but I still didn't want to see it. I rolled my eyes and rubbed my hand across my face. No wonder Cyn wasn't doing her job lately. It would make sense that she spent as much time as she could with Lee lately. They'd just gotten engaged.

"What the hell is wrong with the two of you?" I asked irritably and as loud as I could. "You know you're supposed to be working, both of you. Mom has damn near had it—"

Cynthia's head popped out the door—thankfully fully dressed—her hair tangled and brown eyes wide.

"Shit! I am so sorry. We just kind of got caught up in things and I know I'm supposed to be working but—" Cyn popped her head back into the bedroom and rocked back on her heels. "God, I can't wait to tell anyone. Can I, Lee?"

I refused to look in the bedroom, instead choosing to look at Cynthia in confusion.

"I don't care, baby, do whatever you want to do."

"Lee asked me to move in with him!"

"Ow," I said, taking a step back. She squealed so loud pain shot through my ear. "Do you have to yell?"

"Sorry," she said, wincing, "but I just couldn't help myself! I wanted to wait for a while until I was sure things are okay between us all, but I can't. We want you to be Lee's best man! OH! We want a wedding on the ranch!"

She kept going on and on about the wedding, but all I could think was, "shit."

Chapter Four

Briana

I simply stared at the picture.

I just had twelve week ultrasound. They ran tests to make sure the baby had no birth defects. Everything happened so fast I couldn't keep up with what the ultrasound technician said to me. I was too stunned; too engrossed by the little baby on the screen. Well... it didn't exactly look like a baby yet. It looked more like a bean.

For a moment, the technician thought two babies might be inside, but she dismissed the thought. She was kind of sloppy about the whole thing. All I could do when it happened was sigh in relief. I wasn't pregnant with twins. I could handle one baby, but *two*? No way. I inspected the picture better. From what I could tell, definitely just one baby, but what did I understand about reading that stuff?

I didn't like this hospital. They had outdated equipment and everyone rushed around to get finished as fast as possible. I couldn't afford to go anywhere else.

"You're worrying me."

I glanced at Lora. For all the bitching and lecturing she tried to do in the past few weeks, she was here now, and had given me a ride to my appointment. She gasped when she saw the baby on the screen and held my hand when I wiped a few stray tears from my eyes.

"I'm really pregnant."

"Well, yeah," she said, squeezing my hand. "I thought the first ultrasound you had cleared any doubts up."

"I kind of kept hoping it was a fluke...that maybe the morning sickness was just a stomach bug, or the test was faulty."

"You took three tests. One of them was at the hospital when we took you to get checked out after you fell off the horse. You've had several checkups since to make sure everything is okay."

I shivered as my aunt drove down the road. It was chilly outside, but she had the window cracked open while she smoked a cigarette. Lora didn't care that I was twelve weeks along. Her nicotine was more important. I sat as close to the passenger door as I could so I could stay away from the smoke.

"I know," I said. "I do know that. But I'm allowed to hope it wasn't real, right?"

Lora took a heavy drag off her cigarette. Of all days, it was raining. The freezing cold ice kind of rain. It pinged against the glass on the window shield. She still had her stupid window opened. I shivered and pulled my coat tighter.

"You shouldn't do this. You shouldn't raise a baby yet. You're not ready. I wish you would go over those adoption papers."

"No way," I said. "I'm not giving my baby up."

"You're telling me you hoped you weren't actually pregnant and you expect me to believe you want a baby?" Another drag of the cigarette. "You're making this harder than it has to be."

"Harder?" I pulled my left leg up into the seat and turned to face her. "I'm not fooling myself into thinking this would be easy. Women raise children all the time when they're my age."

"You were in denial about your pregnancy and you're refusing to let Aidan know what happened. If that's not a huge red flag that you're not prepared to be a mother than I don't know what is!"

"You're completely misconstruing my words."

"What else am I supposed to think, Briana? It really sounds like you aren't ready for a baby but you aren't admitting it to yourself."

I huffed again. I hated having these arguments with Lora. Hated it. Half the time I felt like I needed to keep my mouth shut so she wouldn't hear whatever I tried to tell her the wrong way.

"It's nothing," I said, sighing in defeat. She would keep on insisting I think about giving the baby up for adoption, and I would keep fighting with her. We would never get anywhere, never make progress, and stay wrapped around in circles. "I'm tired of fighting. I need some time to get my head together. I'm not naive. Raising a baby is hard. Isn't that enough?"

"No," Lora said. "I'm not convinced."

"I remember everything after Mom had Kevin. I can do this, Lora."

"You were seven when she had him. How can you remember?"

I raised an eyebrow at her. "You try having your little brother pee in your eye and then see if you have trouble remembering such a lovely experience."

Lora sighed then lifted up her butt to pull her cell phone out. "I'm being a little hard on you, aren't I?"

I straightened myself out in the car and leaned my head against the window.

"I realize certain things need to happen now since I have a baby on the way. I do need to tell Aidan, but adoption is totally out of the question. You are being too hard on me. I'm not sure me and Kevin can stay with you if you keep being so rough on me."

I glanced at Lora again. She had her phone propped on top of the steering wheel and as soon as the light turned red, she started typing out a message on the phone. I gaped at her, incredulous. She hadn't bothered to listen to a word I said.

Why did I even expect her to care? She certainly didn't when she went out with some friends to party for New Years. Kevin and I spent the night watching the ball drop. It was nice to spend time with him. I almost worried Lora wouldn't pick me up that morning to take me to my appointment.

"Are you even listening to me?" I asked, reaching for her phone.

"Hey!" Lora said. "Give that back."

"No way. You can't text and drive."

"Don't be ridiculous."

"Forgot your brother died because someone was *texting*, huh?"

Lora froze for a moment. I squealed and grabbed the handle above the door when she floored the gas at the green light and made a sharp turn.

"You know what, honey? I don't even want to deal with this right now."

"What do you mean you don't want to 'deal with it'?" Her phone buzzed in my hand.

"Who is texting me?"

"Some guy named John Bledsoe...?"

"Yep. That right there. We're going to spend some time with him. As adults, not as aunt and niece."

Oh. That kind of 'not dealing with it'.

"Who is he, exactly?"

"He's just a friend."

"Uh huh," I said, handing her phone back. "Sure."

"Honest! Just a friend."

I realized I still held the ultrasound picture in my other hand, so I reached for my purse on the floor and put it inside, all the while trying to gauge my aunt's reaction to me asking about who this John Bledsoe guy was. There was blushing. And adjusting her bra. And more texting. I decided to let that slide for right now. I was with her. I could grab the steering wheel if I needed to. At least she tried to keep the phone on top of the wheel so she could sort of watch the road. The entire process still made me nervous.

"Somehow I don't believe he's only a friend."

"Ugh, okay. We're sort of dating. We used to spend a lot of time together in high school. He had a band."

I couldn't help but laugh. "A band?"

"Yep. Chris and the Mums. They broke up after we all graduated though." She took a left and shoved her phone back into her pocket. "You're okay with me meeting up with him, right? He owns the place."

"No... I guess it's okay," I said. "We won't be long, will we? I promised Kevin a homemade pizza tonight."

"Oh no," Lora said. "I promise we won't be long. I actually want you to meet John. He's an awesome guy."

"Okay," I said, not quite sure what I was getting myself into. "I guess."

Lora laughed and placed her hand on top of mine. "I promise, you'll like him. Rendezvous is my home away from homes. It's where I go when I need to relax. If you get hungry you need to try their chicken wings."

Rendezvous actually turned out to be a pretty decent pub style restaurant. I was shocked by this since we weren't in the best part of town to run business. Too many other places surrounded the pub but it seemed to still attract a decent amount of business despite that it was midday.

"I am so glad you asked me to come over when you did," Lora said, dropping her big clunky purse onto the bar. "I needed to see you!"

She hopped into a bar stool and reached over to grab the man behind the bar by the collar of his shirt, proceeding to give him a big kiss on the cheek.

It wasn't too far-fetched to assume that was John. I looked around the restaurant. The hostess passed us through as soon as she saw Lora, greeting like her like she was an old friend. The display behind the bar was a mixture of old looking oak and glass shelves to hold the liquor. I shook ice out of my hair and decided I didn't like the place.

I studied John for a minute. His jeans were too tight. I knew some men wore women's jeans—why I never could understand—but he definitely struck me as the metrosexual type. His voice was a little high pitched and his ears were gauged with spikes. A line of tattoos traveled down his arm. He was the complete opposite of what I ever imagined my aunt to like as far as her tastes in men went... especially since she was a high school chemistry teacher.

"Want the usual today, sweetie?" he said to my aunt.

Lora looked at me, and then back to John, and shook her head. "No, I think I just want a house ale today. This is my niece, Briana."

John reached for my hand. His hands were softer than mine, but he shook it firmly. He smiled at me wide.

"The pregnant one?"

"John!" Lora smirked.

I had to laugh. "Yeah. I'm the knocked up niece who won't give her baby up for adoption."

"Okay," Lora said, digging in her purse. She pulled the keys out and pressed them into my hand. "I love you, honey, but I'm not comfortable with you being here when you obviously don't want to be."

"Oh, I didn't mean—d—"

"Besides, we shouldn't leave Kevin at home too long by himself," she added.

She was right, even though I felt like I needed to point out that she didn't need to send me home.

"How are you going to get home?"

I couldn't just leave her without at least knowing that.

"I'll give her a ride home," John said. "You don't need to worry."

I studied him for a second, not sure if I should trust him. It wasn't because of the tattoos or the piercings. No—I would never dream of judging someone because they chose to decorate their body with art. It was because I never met him before.

But I was tired. My feet hurt because I needed new flats and the ones I had on had a hole forming around my left big toe.

I sighed. "Okay. I'll catch up with you later, Lora."

Aidan

I took a long gulp of beer while a woman I never met before eyed me and Bobby. She swayed on her feet. Throughout the night she ordered more than one drink. Every time she came to the bar, she ogled us. We were here to celebrate Cyn and Lee's engagement; not to attract the attention of strange women. At first, I hadn't wanted to, but as best man I felt obligated, damn it. I had a serious case of third-party syndrome until I called Bobby and asked him if he wanted to drink a couple beers with me.

Samantha, at work for the night, wanted to talk with us but she was close to being swamped because of the Friday night dinner rush.

I ignored the woman even when she brushed her hand against my arm.

"Look, sorry sweetheart, but me and my buddy aren't interested."

I couldn't help it. I had to glance at her on that one. The girl raised her eyebrow comically.

"Are the two of you a couple?"

She had a high pitched voice that almost made her sound like a dog's squeak toy.

"No, honey," Samantha said behind the bar. "I'm this one's girlfriend." She pointed to Bobby before she leaned across the bar and kissed Bobby soundly on the mouth. "That one isn't available either."

I burst out laughing. The girl's eyes widened, she grabbed her drink, and stormed off.

"There you all are."

I tensed immediately at the sound of my ex-girlfriend's voice. Odd, I realized, because I came to celebrate her engagement to my cousin. But the entire thing was weird, especially since I used to think I would be the one to end up marrying her.

I'd barely said much to them since we decided we wanted a couple of drinks. Other than agreeing to be Lee's best man, I didn't know what else to say to him because of the fact that I walked in on him having sex with Cynthia. It was the last thing I needed to see that day, and now it was seven P.M.

"Samantha? Can I have something a little stronger? Bourbon." I pulled money out of my wallet and offered it to her.

Cynthia and Lee sat next to us.

Samantha smacked the bar top and nodded. "Sure thing, Aidan." She slid my money back to me. "This round is on the house. I'll give all of you the good stuff."

"Oh, does that mean I can have a Long Island Ice Tea?"

Samantha hesitated.

"You *sure* you want one of those?"

Cynthia rolled her eyes. "Yeah, duh."

"All right. I guess so."

"I fucking *love* you."

I had to laugh at Cyn. Her mood became infectious. I hadn't seen her so happy in a long time.

"I hear someone got engaged."

Cynthia shot up so fast out of her stool and up onto the bar she almost knocked her elbow into my jaw. Thankfully I had quick reflexes and pulled away in time.

"Yeah." She held out her left hand. "Isn't it pretty?"

"Christ on a cracker," I said, "be careful, Sinner."

Cynthia flipped me the bird.

"You know what, why don't you come on back here? I'll teach you how to make your drink. Let the boys talk some," Samantha said.

"Okay!" Cyn said.

It was a little strange those two were getting along.

Women were difficult creatures who would never make sense to men. I still couldn't figure out why Briana decided to move and why I couldn't get a hold of her. I missed her like crazy but I refused to beg Nikki to tell me where she was anymore. It made me feel like a pathetic idiot.

"You're a dick," Bobby said to Lee.

"What the hell am I a dick for?" Lee asked.

"Now I need to ask Samantha to marry me and we're not ready."

"Dude, aren't you like in your mid-thirties?"

"You say that, but what the hell are you thinking asking Cynthia Lesikar to marry you? That girl isn't going to be happy tied down to one man. I told Aidan that when he started dating her, and I'm telling it to you now. She's not wife material even though I love her to death."

Cynthia heard him. She merely stuck her tongue out. She'd heard Bobby's spiels about her before whenever he got drunk. It used to bother her but now it was just how he chose to pick on her.

"I'm staying out of this one," I laughed.

Lee opened his mouth to say something, but changed his mind, and instead took a drink of his beer.

"So I hear you're thinking about moving into Grandma's old house."

I glanced up at him, not expecting that one. I'd briefly mentioned to Mom that I wanted—no needed—a bigger place. I had too many memories there and I felt like I needed to start fresh somewhere. I hear to make a fresh start you need to move. Apparently, that was more the type of thing Briana did.

"Yeah," I said. "I'm thinking about fixing the house up. No one has been living in it and we need to make sure it doesn't go to waste. Mom promised me part of the ranch for my inheritance when I turned eighteen but she needed the extra money so she rented the house out."

"It's a fucking mess," Lee said. "I stopped over there to check it out and I can't see why Aunt Abs let those people trash it the way they did without suing them."

"I think it's about time you move somewhere that isn't a hole in the wall," Bobby said.

I took a drink of my beer. "You've got that wrong," I said. "Cynthia is the one who lives in a hole in the wall. Her bedroom doesn't even have windows. I have an actual apartment."

"What do you plan on doing about that lease you have on it though?" Lee asked. "I know your rental company can be real dick heads when it comes to breaking them."

"That's not a problem," I said, shrugging. "I can easily find a college student to take over the lease."

"Might work," Bobby said. "But I have seen the place. It needs a lot of work. Can you afford to fix it up?"

I shrugged. "Mom told me she'll help me pay for whatever I need help with as long as I fix it, you know?"

"Yeah, but you'll need to like, hire people to fix shit. That can get expensive, man."

"Why the fuck would I hire someone? I'll get you clowns to help me fix the house up."

Bobby and Lee took one look at each other and then burst into laughter.

They didn't realize I was serious.

Chapter Five

Aidan

Valentine's Day was in two weeks.

I still heard nothing from Briana and I was damn near done.

I hated thinking that way. I loved her. Hell, I just wanted to know if she was okay. I gave up the idea of getting Lora to tell me anything. I didn't want her causing any trouble by having her get pissed and claim I was harassing her. I briefly thought about calling Kevin but ultimately decided against not to. Briana didn't want to be a part of my life anymore. With Lora so aggressively protective, I couldn't blame anyone but myself for not being clearer when I realized I wanted a relationship with Bri.

I shook my head at myself, instead focusing on Cynthia's apartment door. I had to wait for her since her mother still needed to borrow her car. Mom insisted Lee stay busy on the ranch so he couldn't pick her up and neither one of us wanted her to walk to class in the snow currently dusting the front of my mother's truck. I need to pick up a few things for the horses anyway while I was in town, so it made sense to offer her a ride while I was still out here.

"I'm freezing," Cyn said, throwing her backpack onto the floorboard. She reached for me and I pulled her up. She never could successfully climb into Mom's truck. She started rubbing her hands together as soon as she was in. "It's fucking cold out there. My heater in my apartment fucked up."

"Shit," I said. I reached over and put the heater on high. "Here, see if that helps."

The poor thing shook when she reached for the heater vent. Cyn always hated cold weather. I couldn't remember how many times she cuddled up to me on the way to the stables even though it made it hard to walk because she was cold while we still dated.

"Yeah, thanks." She crossed her arms and rubbed them. "Burr. I'm mad at Lee for not picking me up."

"Don't say that," I said. "Mom has him busy with the horses. They need to make sure everything would be secure for the night so they would be warm."

Cynthia shrugged. "I know." She pulled her phone from her pocket and looked at the time. "I don't want Lee to drive in this weather anyway. He doesn't know how to drive the truck and his car is as bad as yours is in snow."

I scoffed. "My car can handle the snow fine."

Cynthia raised an eyebrow. "I seem to remember a time when you backed into a ditch sometime about two years ago and needed to use a shovel and a wooden block to get the car out."

I rolled my eyes.

I hated when she mentioned me getting my car stuck. It still embarrassed the fuck out of me to this day.

"Don't," I said. "Especially if you don't want to walk to class."

"You wouldn't dare," she said.

"You know I will."

"You're a dick. That's why things would have never worked with us."

I knew she was joking but I couldn't help but frown at her. Cyn huffed in response and I pulled out of the parking lot.

"Change in subject," I said. "We've both been busy the past couple of weeks. How are things going with your new roommate?"

"It's okay. She's definitely not Briana. She leaves her shampoo everywhere—"

I braked too hard.

The truck slid a couple feet but I managed to stop in time so we didn't pull onto the main road.

"Holy shit!" Cyn grabbed for the dashboard. "Be careful. I would like to get to class in one piece!"

"Sorry," I said, a little shaken too. "Don't mention Briana out of the blue."

"It's been over two months," she said. "You're still not over her?"

"What am I supposed to say? She moved for no reason, so yeah, I am having trouble dealing because I have no idea if she's okay or not."

"How do you think I feel about it? I have no idea where she is either. Fuck, her stupid futon and a couple other things Nikki didn't bother to pack up are still in my apartment. Nikki refuses to fess up."

"I gave up a while ago trying to get Nikki to tell me anything. She's keeping her mouth sealed shut. I wish I knew if it was something I did wrong."

"You didn't," Cynthia said.

A huge wave of confusion and suspicion washed through me. "What does supposed to mean?"

I was driving and the roads weren't been salted yet so I didn't chance a glance at her. The thing about dating someone as long as I did is we didn't need to make eye contact for me to know she tensed up.

"It means something. Do you have any idea why Bri left?"

I chanced a look at her.

"I don't know anything, Aidan." She released a nervous laugh. "Why would I? She moved back to Kentucky. That's the last I heard about her. She's an adult and doesn't need an explanation for why; I'm betting it was the wild hair she forgot to pull out of her ass."

"Cyn," I scolded. "Come on, don't."

"Well I'm sorry, I'm tired of watching you mope around. You won't go on a date with my new roommate, and honestly I don't blame you, but you should still try going on a date with one of my friends."

"I'm not letting you do that to me again. It never turns out well."

Cynthia huffed. "You're so difficult."

"I don't want to date, period."

"No, you want to pout and become an asshole since you aren't getting laid. Bitching at me for not being able to carry two bales of hay like some kind of She-Hulk? Seriously, Aidan?"

"You normally don't have a problem with it."

"Not when it's warm! When it's freezing, I'd like to be sure I'm not going to slip and fall on my ass."

"And I don't need to get laid."

"Yes you do! I have a friend who really wants to meet you."

"You have fixed me up before. It never works, Cynthia. I'm trusting my gut, and dating right now isn't healthy."

Cynthia made a little indignant huff and turned down the radio. "Just because one girl took off you aren't going to give another one a chance? Briana left in November, Aidan. It's been long enough. I think you need at least a rebound fuck."

"Cyn," I said. "I don't want to go on a date with anyone."

"She's got red hair and she used to be a cheerleader."

Stop light. I groaned. Cynthia knew I had a soft spot for fucking red heads. That's the reason my interested in Briana piqued in the beginning. Honestly I had thought about dating for a while but knew I wasn't ready.

"She can bend her legs way far back behind her head and—"

"You're not going to get me to take a girl out. I'm done letting you fix me up."

"Don't be a stubborn ass! I've talked about you constantly. I haven't really known this girl too long. I kind of think she doesn't count on the me 'fixing you up with one of my friends' thing."

"You're talking to a girl who you're not close to about me? Great, Cyn. I'm I love how you're trying to pimp me out again."

"I am doing no such thing."

"That's exactly what you did with Briana. And Jamie way before we ever met her, even though I didn't go out with her because I was still trying to get used to the whole open relationship concept."

"Come on," Cyn said in a whiny voice. "I can't date like I used to so I need to live vicariously through you."

"No you don't!" I said. "Why don't you live vicariously with your fiancé?"

"Lee isn't romantic like you are. Usually it's just, 'hey, want to go get a burger?' I fucking hate fast food... Except Taco Bell. Taco Bell is awesome."

"He's just trying to save money for the wedding."

Cynthia sighed. "Dad sucks because he's being a dick head and doesn't want to pay for it. He thinks I should move back up north and let him introduce me to one of his lawyer buddy's sons. I'm sorry, I don't want a city boy. I want my country man. Men are sexier when they can rope a horse instead of argue about the stock market."

We both looked at each other at the same time and started laughing. I once experienced how her father hounded her to date men he deemed more appropriate first hand. We were together, and happy, and it wasn't a pretty sight once I got pissed at him. At least we could truly laugh about it now.

"Oh man, I needed that," Cynthia said after a few minutes. She clutched her sides. "Make sure you don't miss the turn onto campus."

It was really hard to laugh so hard my sides started to hurt, but still try to keep the truck on the road. "Yeah, I'm not planning on missing it."

"Well you please think about going on a date with the girl? I promise she's nice."

I sighed. I knew I wouldn't get out of it. Cyn was relentless when she wanted something. That's probably why she had a diamond engagement ring on her finger from my cousin and why I was never able to say no to her before when we dated.

"When am I supposed to take her on this date?"

"In like two weeks... on Valentine's Day."

I almost slammed my foot on the breaks a second time.

"Are you kidding me?" I asked her. "No way. I don't like all of that commercial holiday shit."

"Aidan!"

"Your whiny voice shit will not work on me for this. No."

"But she is expecting you to be at Mama's Pizzeria that day!"

"You already set up the fucking date?"

Cyn sat up straighter and removed her seat belt. I parked next to the building where her class was.

"I know you can't say *no* to me."

"That's where you're wrong. We're not in a relationship anymore."

"Come on, I feel bad because things didn't work out with Bri."

I sighed, scrubbed my hand over my face. "Fine. If I go out with her can we ban all talk about Bri?"

"Yes," Cyn said, nodding her head enthusiastically. "We can ban all talk about her."

"Fine, I guess I'll go out on a date."

"Awesome."

"Fuck, are we teenagers again?"

Cynthia laughed again. "No, we aren't, but you are going to make a girl's night when you show up for the date with a rose and some chocolate." She fake gasped. "You might even get laid!"

I didn't really know what to say to that so I decided to leave it alone.

Briana

I didn't like Kevin's principal.

I crossed my arms, then uncrossed them, and my brother took my hand. I wanted to blow up at everyone in the office and his touch reminded me to keep my cool. I needed to try to be professional.

"Let me get this straight," I said. A kid a little older than Kevin sat next to his mother, a light-blonde haired woman who glared at me harshly with crossed arms. He got off far worse than Kevin, with a black eye, he would need stitches in his busted lip. Kevin had not one scratch on him. "My brother took it upon himself to kick your ass because you decided to be *cool* and pick on a girl?"

So much for professionalism. Kevin released my hand to muffle his laugh.

"Excuse me!" the mother said, standing straighter. "You will not talk to my son like that!"

"My brother did nothing wrong," I said, standing too. The girl in question sat in the hallway with her head down on her knees while she cried softly. I noticed her when I walked into Principal Robinson's office, stunned when I realized Kevin decided to stand up to one of the most popular football players in the school.

The kid was probably a sophomore and but lacked the better sense not to mess with a girl half his size; just from looking at him, he lacked many brain cells.

"Bri, *calm down...*" Kevin said.

"No, I won't," I hissed, looking down at him. "I'm proud of you for defending that girl."

"If we could all take a seat," Principal Robinson said. Her pursed lips gave me the impression that she sucked on lemons too often. "I don't quite believe that is what happened."

"Kevin was hitting on the girl and she didn't like his advances," the kid said. "It was me who defended her."

"Oh that is a load of *bullshit*," I said.

I never wanted to punch a more uppity bitch in my entire life. Ever since I arrived in the office, she threw accusations at Kevin. I wouldn't take that. I would home school him before I let that happen.

"Briana, calm down," Kevin said. "Please, you're pregnant."

"Seriously? You're *pregnant*?" the woman laughed and looked at Principal Robinson. "How old is this girl? Eighteen? I would like to speak to your parents."

"I'm twenty-one," I said. "Our parents passed away a few years ago."

If it didn't hurt to admit our parents passed away, her shocked expression would have been priceless. Her shock didn't last long. "No wonder her brother is getting into fights. She's completely unprepared to parent a teenager."

Seriously. Tempted. To. Punch. Her. In. The. Face.

"Isn't there a legal custodian of this child?"

"In case you didn't listen to me, I'm it."

"Ladies," the principal said, standing.

"I may be young and pregnant, but I've obviously done better with my brother for the past *four* years than you have with your son for the past *sixteen*." Kevin bit his fist and laughed when I motioned for him to stand up. I wrapped my arms around him and had to wonder again when he grew taller than me. "I'm proud of you. Introduce me to this girl?"

"Doesn't this kid have an aunt who works here?"

I turned around quickly. "She's not his sole caregiver. I am." I shook my head and placed my hand on the Kevin's shoulder. "Let's get out here."

The angry mother started to say something else but Mrs. Robinson said, "Let it go, Mrs. Freeman. We need to talk about how this is the fourth time your son has harassed a female student."

"Robin," Kevin said. "Are you okay?"

Robin sniffed and looked up. She still hugged her knees. She was a pretty girl, with pitch black hair that fell in loose curls around her face. I think the most striking thing about her was the streak of bright blue that fell down in one of the curls. She wore a Black Sabbath t shirt and worn blue jeans.

She wiped her face. "Yeah. I think."

Kevin sat down next to her. "I'm sorry he talked to you like that."

"You didn't need to get into a fight for me," Robin said.

"You shouldn't ever let someone call you a slut. You aren't," Kevin said.

"I've been called worse."

"That's not even the worst thing he said to you. I can't believe you were about to just take it—"

"Yeah, but I didn't want you in trouble. I asked you to stay out of it."

The last thing I wanted to do was interrupt them but I had an important check up with the doctor, so I cleared my throat. "Care to introduce me, Kev?" I asked.

"Oh," Kevin said, "Robin, this is my sister, Bri. Bri, this is Robin Jones."

She waved at me meekly, her face turning red when she realized I was standing there.

"Hi," she said.

"I heard some of the things that kid said to you...You shouldn't take that, sweetie."

Robin shrugged. "I'm used to it," she said to me. Then she turned to Kevin. "You did get in trouble, didn't you?"

"Three day suspension." Kevin shrugged.

I looked at the time on my phone and sighed. "We need to get going. It was nice to meet you, Robin."

"You too," Robin said.

Kevin sighed. He looked like he wanted to hug her, or stay at school with her, but I'd already signed him out before I found out about his suspension.

"Come to dinner tonight," Kevin blurted. Then he turned red. "She can come to dinner, right, Bri?"

I couldn't help but smile at them.

My little brother liked a girl close to his own age.

No way would I let him live it down.

Aidan

I stood in front of my grandparent's old house, key in my hand, debating on whether I wanted to go inside or not.

I hadn't thought about this place in a long time.

I seriously considered moving. Mom offered once before, but I turned her down because I wanted my own place. It was enough that I worked for Mom on the ranch, I didn't want to live where I worked too. Now that I was older, with straighter priorities, I realized wouldn't mind living on the ranch, nor I waste money on rent if I lived here.

I needed a project. Sure, working on the ranch with the horses helped, but I needed a distraction.

Mom and I briefly talked about me moving onto the ranch a few years ago after she last evicted the family that rented this place. A lot of history came with the house for our family, with at least four generations, including Mom and her mother. I could already tell I would need to sand down the porch and patch up a few holes around the foundation. A window next to the front door was busted in. I chased a couple kids off our property a few months ago because they thought an abandoned house would be a good place to hang out. Mom loved lecturing them in front of their parents but she didn't press their parents to pay for the damages when I thought she needed to. The house needed a lot of work but I could conjure up a vision of it when I finished remodeling. I wanted to move the fence closer so the horses could be near. I would love watching Blue Moon graze while I drank coffee in the morning.

I could make this my home.

Living in the apartment would only work for so long.

Mom only used the house for storage now. She sent me out here with the intent of moving things around to see what I needed to do.

Paint. That was the first thing going on my list. I made a note on my phone. Everything was peeling and the outside of the house needed to be sanded down. I figured Mom would take better care of the house because she wanted me to eventually move in, but at the same time she was busy doing a lot of other things on the ranch. Dad was useless when it came to doing anything useful here since he ran his own business and never cared for the horses. If it were up to him, he would sell everything. I initially considered hiring someone to do the work but the money would come out of the funds that went into running the ranch and Mom wasn't willing to spend an arm and a leg to pay someone professional. I either did the repairs by myself or I couldn't move in.

I wasn't even sure if I wanted to move out yet. It was just something I thought about. I couldn't be in my house without thinking about everything that went down with Briana and Cynthia. It wasn't that I missed what I had with either one of the girls either. Hell no. I missed nothing about my open relationship with Cyn. She was engaged to my cousin now. I was happy for them. Shit, Lee asked me to be his best man. Telling myself that I didn't miss Briana felt easier. I couldn't dwell on how shitty it really was now that she wasn't around any longer, or how damn bad she hurt me by taking off the way she did.

"Are you just going to stand there all day or are you going inside?"

I turned to see Cynthia at the edge of the steps with Rhiannon. The two of them had taken off about an hour ago for a ride to give lessons to kids from Mom's church group. She reached forward and slowly ran her hand through the horse's mane but remained in the saddle as she looked at me.

"Since when do you blow off giving riding lessons?" I asked her.

"I wasn't feeling it today. Aberlie knew that." Cyn shrugged. "What are you doing over here anyway? This place is old and falling apart. What do your parents even use it for? Storage or something?"

"I thought you knew," I said.

"Nah. I still try to stay out of your mother's way. She's not entirely happy with me being engaged to Lee."

I had to laugh at her.

"You know you don't give Mom enough credit, right?"

"She and I don't exactly see eye to eye."

I shook my head and finally opened the front door. "I'm thinking about moving in here."

I could hear Cyn dismount. Pretty sure she was going to tie the reins to the porch, I walked further in the house. I could see where mom kept most of her things she wanted for storage piled in a corner. All of us were busy so I hadn't expected them to be in perfect condition. Mostly she stored old books and electronics. I spotted my old Nintendo poking out of a box that I'd taken away from the teenagers who tried to break in.

"You are?" Cyn asked. "But you love your bachelor pad and wasting money on rent every month."

I turned to her with a raised eyebrow. "Really? Bachelor pad?"

"Yep."

"I don't enjoy paying rent, Cyn."

"I was afraid to set foot inside the other day when you asked me and Lee to watch a movie. You've like...*totally* stopped cleaning. It's *so* gross."

I rolled my eyes. "Gross" to Cynthia was forgetting to wash a couple of dishes and not making my bed. My place wasn't perfect but I usually tried to keep things in order.

I just didn't want to be at home often. The apartment no longer felt like home. I'd been spending a lot of time with Briana, and before that, Cynthia. I'd never had a place to myself that was solely mine while I was single. I still found Cyn's crap all over the place. Which was one of the reasons I wanted her to come over with Lee; so we could spend time together and I could send her home with a box of her shit. Her things slowly trailed their way into Mom's house and Lee's bedroom since they announced their engagement.

"Why don't you get a place with Lee?"

Cyn shrugged and walked past me. She ran her hand along a cardboard box, deep in thought, like she wasn't sure how to answer my question.

"You do want to live with him, right?"

"Yeah, I do," she said. "It's just that we're not actually married yet, you know? So I don't feel like we need to move in together."

"I've thought about talking to him about taking my place," I shrugged. "I naturally assumed you might move in with him."

"Ah, I'm not sure." She shrugged again before changing the subject. "Are you ready for your date?"

I groaned. "Are you seriously going to force me into taking out a girl I never met before?"

"I absolutely am," Cyn chirped. "Paige is a really great girl. I think you'll like her."

"I'd rather work on this place all night than go on a date."

"Aidan! I'm marrying your cousin and I'm happy and if you don't go on a date with my friend then I might just have a bridezilla moment 'cause she's one of my bridesmaids!"

Suddenly, it all made sense.

"Are you kidding me?"

She looked down and shifted from one foot to the other. "No. I'm not kidding. I'm thinking about asking Paige to be my maid of honor."

"And I'm Lee's best man."

"Yep."

"Did it ever occur to you that if this date goes bad then it may make things *awkward* at the wedding?"

"Aidan! Just do this for me! I want you guys to like meet up and see if anything sparks. If it doesn't Paige will understand. I haven't asked her to fill in for that anyway yet. But Lee and I are wanting to get married pretty fast without it totally being an elopement so..."

Lee didn't want to get married fast. *Cynthia* wanted to get married fast. Lee just acted like he wanted to, too. If he didn't put his foot down they'd be married in two weeks. I had to swallow back the chuckle at the thought. Cynthia always knew what she wanted, and that had been something I once loved about her, even though she had a tendency to become overbearing.

"Can't you just have a dinner party with the people you want in your wedding like a normal person?"

"Nope. I'm not normal...you haven't figured that out yet?"

I hadn't, and for my cousin's sake, I hoped he would learn it eventually.

I ran my hand along the edge of the nearest window, trying to discern what kind of shape the interior of the house was in. The paint chipped almost immediately. Cynthia said something else but I ignored her, more intent on inspecting the house to decide if I could actually do something with it. It would be useless to move in if the place would only turn into a money pit in the end.

"Aidan, are you even listening to me?"

I jumped, not expecting her to yell at me so loud, and turned quickly.

Big mistake. The window I'd been inspecting was the one the kids broke when they decided to explore the house, and my hand slid right across the glass like butter.

"Fuck!" I hissed.

In a matter of seconds, Cynthia grabbed my hand. "Could you be any clumsier?"

"Well if you didn't holler, rant, and rave at me when I stopped listening to you then maybe I wouldn't have cut my damn hand!" I ripped my arm away from her. A solid stream of blood ran over my wrist. I hissed, spreading the cut out a little. I couldn't tell if it'd gone down to the bone or not, but I definitely had a gash in the web between my thumb and index finger.

"If you'd listen I wouldn't have to yell! My god, you never listened to me."

"Whatever, Cynthia," I said.

"You probably need stitches."

"Go bother your fiancé."

"No way! I'm taking you to the damn hospital."

"I'm not going."

"Stubborn ass, do you want an infection?"

"I'm not your problem anymore."

"I'll tell your mother."

Well, fuck.

"All right, damn it." She made a move to look at my hand again and I yanked it back, pointing my finger from my good hand at her. "No, Ms. Grabby Paws. I know you're all eager and shit to do stitches or whatever the fuck it is they're prepping you for at Bobby's clinic, but I'm human, and I'll drive my own damn self to the hospital."

"But that looks pretty—"

"You need to get back to the trail riding. Tell Mom and Lee where I went."

Briana

I hated the way women looked at me when I came to the hospital for my appointment. They knew by now that I didn't like any of them, but I was stuck coming here if I wanted a healthy pregnancy unless I wanted to travel a few hours out of town. But, being eighteen weeks pregnant, it was inevitable. I hated the drive out of town to get the ultrasound done but I didn't like any of the practices closer to Lora's house, either.

Hopefully, I'd find out the sex of my baby. I was jittery and nervous all at the same time to find out, and upset with Lora because she wouldn't be there for me to see. They tried to find out last time but the baby wouldn't turn around.

"Do I have to sit in here for this?"

"No," I said, knowing my brother hated being in the hospital with me, "but you're going to stay here and wait anyway."

"Bri!" Kevin whined, shifting uncomfortably in his seat. "This isn't fair."

"I'm mad at you," I said. "So you get to see the baby with me."

"It's weird. I can't believe that woman asked you so many questions about how far along you and wanted to feel your stomach. You're not even huge yet."

I ran my hand across my stomach, ignoring my brother's comment. I'm sure the baby started fluttering. At first I thought it was gas and complained to my doctor, but she assured me that the baby could be moving.

"Miss King?"

The ultrasound technician, I'd forgotten her name, came in with a wide smile.

"Hi," I said, adjusting myself on the stiff bed. I hated this part but at the same time I was too excited to see the baby. "Please tell me I don't have to get any blood work done today."

I'd recently discovered how much I hated needles. Just the thought of them made me uncomfortable. I shivered a little at the thought of it from the last time I had to get blood drawn because they couldn't find one of my veins.

The ultrasound technician took a seat next to the bed, smiling while she shook her head. "No, we don't need to draw any blood. In two weeks we'll have you come back to talk to Doctor Monroe to discuss anything you're worried about, get your weight, stuff like that. Pull your shirt up for me?"

Kevin cleared his throat next to us.

"You are?" the woman asked.

"Oh, I'm the uncle," he said.

"This is his punishment for getting suspended from school for fighting."

"Ahh," she said, a bit of mirth now in her tone,

I wiggled my jeans down a little so she could spread more of the cool jelly on my stomach.

"Why don't you come over here? Don't you want to see the baby?" I asked, turning my head toward my brother.

"This is strange."

"Will you stop being a big baby?"

The ultrasound technician laughed and lightly moved the wand over my stomach.

The baby appeared, and more than ever I wished I could just get over myself and let Aidan know.

"Oh my gosh," I said as soon as its little body appeared, legs kicking and wiggling, but all I could really see was what looked like its back. I turned my head back to Kevin. "Come on, aren't at least a little curious?"

Kevin kept his head turned away, completely intent on not looking at the baby. I rolled my eyes and turned my head back to the monitor. I could feel it a little, confirming that I hadn't actually been gassy the past few weeks.

"There's the head," the technician said, laughing. "Though I don't know that we'll get a good look at the face." She continued to press keys and capture some pictures, like small stills of its head. "I'm going to measure your belly."

"Can you tell me if it's a boy or girl?"

She grinned at me. "Yeah, I can, if it will ever stop wiggling!"

"Is it normal for them to be so active?"

I felt like that was such a dumb question, but as a first time mom, I had no idea what in the world I was getting myself into. Lora was right, in some aspects, that I was unprepared to become a mother to a newborn. I didn't have a job and my own place, and my brother was still in school, and he depended on me.

The technician spent a few minutes trying to get the baby to turn around, but it wouldn't keep its legs still long enough, and wouldn't turn, so we could get a good view of its bottom. I had to laugh because I could already tell I'd have a stubborn child on my hands, just like its father, and more than anything it reminded me how much I missed Aidan. I suddenly wished that I hadn't run the way that I had, that I could get up the courage to call him. I felt so stupid for changing my number.

I couldn't let him know yet, though. I had to get my head on straight. I had to make sure I could really handle becoming a mom to a baby, and I had to figure out what I would do with myself now that college would obviously need to be put on hold.

"That's amazing..." Kevin said, dragging me out of my thoughts. "I'm really going to be an uncle."

He grabbed my hand and scooted as close as he could, like he couldn't get close enough to see the baby. My heart soared a little, and I wondered when I'd become such a sap, because it made me want to cry since Kevin seemed so invested in seeing the baby.

"You are," I said.

"This is so crazy."

The ultrasound technician huffed at my question, and moved the wand some more. "You have a very active baby, and it's perfectly fine. You want this kind of activity."

"Okay," I said, sighing a breath of relief.

"The baby must be shy," Kevin joked, eagerly watching the screen. "I want to know if it's a boy or girl just as bad as you do."

"It just won't stop kicking," the technician said, shaking her head with a chuckle.

Kevin perked up a little, patting my hand until I turned his way.

"What?" I asked, maybe in too much of an annoyed, sisterly tone.

"Maybe you should get up and jump around a little to get the baby to move."

I looked at the technician, then back at my brother, and rolled my eyes. "Don't be ridiculous."

I ended up jumping up and down, feeling like a total fool the entire time even though I giggled my head off.

It worked.

He turned to face us.

I needed to get over myself. Aidan and I would be parents to a little boy. I wanted to—needed—to tell him, but that was so much easier said than done.

~*~

Aidan

All our crap little town had was a band aide station, so I ripped up a piece of my shirt, tied it tight around my hand, and drove myself to the hospital about twenty minutes out of town. They had a decent emergency room even though they were small. The cut looked deep but thankfully I hadn't sliced any important veins.

I'd been in the waiting room for almost five minutes.

"You're a damn fool."

Mom sat next to me, red faced and hair all over the place. She pulled a soft drink out of her purse then slung it to the ground.

"I told Cynthia to tell you I'm fine!"

"Like hell you're fine," Mom said. "Let me see your hand."

I moved it out of the way so she wouldn't grab my wrist.

"The doctor will stitch me up."

"You should've driven to the one in town."

"They suck," I said. "They suck so bad my insurance doesn't cover treatment at their facility."

"I keep telling you to switch to a damn PPO," Mom griped.

"Look, you don't have to be—"

I stopped, staring at the back of a girl with red hair down to her waist. She had a kid standing next to her with the same color hair. I thought about getting up, seeing if maybe it was—

No, it couldn't be Briana.

"Aidan McCoy?"

I didn't have much time to think about the red headed girl, too worried about my hand to see if it had really been her.

She moved to Kentucky and changed her number. Done deal. I needed to stop stressing myself out over every little detail about my ex-lover.

~*~

Briana

After the ultrasound, and finding out I would be having a boy in a few short months, Kevin and I decided to make a trip to the grocery store. I felt like celebrating by indulging myself on my favorite snack lately—beef jerky. I also needed to get a few things to make for dinner. I tried calling Lora, but she didn't answer me, so frustration started to set in because I had no idea where she'd gone.

"Am I forgiven yet? I sat through the ultrasound."

"I'm so happy you sat through it with me but I'm still mad at you for getting in trouble. Fighting in school, really? You can defend your friend's honor in other ways."

I had us parked in the local grocery store lot. I'd been in the mood to experiment with healthier food lately, and with home cooking, rather than eating out all the time. Lora wanted me to stay home. She finally backed off on the adoption thing and told me it was okay if I didn't want to work so I started to think about what I would do after I gave birth.

"What else was I supposed to do? I couldn't just sit there and let that jerk hurt Robin."

I looked at my brother. Really, I studied him, and realized for the first time that all the worrying Lora and I did about him not being mature enough to take care of himself may have been us acting too overprotective. He was a young man now. He defended a girl's honor and even though he got in trouble. I had no reason to be mad at him.

"You like this girl, don't you?" His pink cheeks said everything. "How come I never heard about her before?"

Kevin refused to make eye contact. Even his neck changed color when he got embarrassed.

He cleared his throat. "You were preoccupied before with your own drama."

"You've got a point," I said, agreeing. "I got busy. I've been a crappy sister for a while, huh?"

"No way," Kevin said, turning toward me and grabbing my hand. "You've never been a crappy sister. Why would you think that?"

"It's just that I haven't exactly been there for you...I've been caught up in my own drama and I forgot that you might still need me sometimes."

"You'd be a crappy sister if you wouldn't have given up your college life to raise me when Mom and Dad died... but you did. I might not have appreciated it then, but I do now." He sounded genuinely upset, like maybe I'd offended him. "Don't ever call yourself a crappy sister. You're not and I hate it when you ask me if you are."

"It's just...I wasn't there for you. That's the definition of a crappy sister, Kevin."

"You're here for me now. That's all that matters."

We stared at each other for a minute. My brother was turning into a man and I realized it was about time I started recognized it.

"Is Robin your girlfriend?"

I'd been super emotional lately. I wasn't sure why, but it was just better to change the subject before I got too upset and made Kevin uncomfortable.

"No...But I think I want her to be."

"She looks hardcore, but she's cute."

"I think she just does that because she gets picked on so bad at school. She's really sweet."

"Hey, there's nothing wrong with dying your hair and wearing black."

"I think it's cool."

"She did seem sweet," I said, agreeing with his earlier statement. "Didn't you invite her to dinner?

Kevin turned redder. We both got out of the car.

"I did... but now I don't want to subject her to Lora."

I smiled at him, not quite sure how to react to that.

"I'm sure Lora wouldn't do that to you."

"You haven't been around the past few months," Kevin said.

"Oh my god, Briana?"

I froze in front of the shopping carts. Something—glass—crashed to the ground.

Nikki stared at me, her mouth open wide, a bag of groceries on the concrete at her feet.

"Nikki? What are you doing here?"

"My parents live in this town... Duh. What the hell are you doing here? I thought you moved to Kentucky!"

Kevin looked at me, rolled his eyes, and went inside of the store.

I had a lot of explaining to do.

Chapter Six

Briana

"I can't believe this! You're living in Tennessee?!"

"I—Well—"

"I've been worried about you for weeks. Lora wouldn't tell me how to contact you."

"Nikki, I can explain, I—"

"God, some friend you are!"

Nikki turned so fast I barely had time to recover from my shock so I could run after her.

"Wait!"

"Nice to know you can drop your friends whenever you decide you want to forget everyone!"

"That's not what it is at all!"

"Oh, I forgot, you're pregnant! All the more reason to alienate yourself from your best friend!"

"That's not what happened and you know it!"

Nikki turned around so quick I almost ran into her.

"Then what happened, huh? Other than that I just dropped twenty dollars of groceries on the ground?"

The broken eggs and busted milk jug on the ground made me feel horrible.

"I can buy you more."

"Whatever," Nikki said, turning around. "Keep your money. You need it more."

"I didn't know what to do, okay!?"

She threw her hands up in frustration. "I don't see how that's my problem, Briana. You shut me out when you didn't call me as soon as you knew you were staying in Tennessee!"

She whipped around and started to leave.

I didn't care I was pregnant. I grabbed her arm even though right now she was hurt and she probably wanted kind to kick my ass. "Will you stop for a minute so I can talk to you?"

"No! You didn't even give Aidan the courtesy, so why should I?" She reached over to touch my stomach, her eyes went wide at the small bulge. I pulled away, weirdly violated by the invasion of my personal space. "A small bump. I guess he still has no idea?"

"What am I supposed to do, Nikki? I don't think he wants to be a father. I need to watch out for myself and this baby first."

"You are so, *so* wrong." Nikki shook her head. "You know what? I'm washing my hands of this. It's none of my business. If you want to throw away one of the best guys you ever met, go *right* ahead. He's *heartbroken.*"

Talk about a slap in the face.

"He is?" I asked in a small voice.

"Well I don't know, I haven't actually spoken to him. I've talked to Lee, though, and he's said Aidan is absolutely beside himself even though he won't talk to anyone about it."

Both of us started crying.

"You broke my heart too. You changed your number and never responded to any of my emails or anything. What gives you the right to drop off the face of the planet, Bri?"

"Lora thinks I need time to myself," I said, sobbing. "What am I supposed to do? Having a baby scares the hell out of me."

"Woman up! Pull up your big girl panties and stop hiding like a child. Is that what you're going to do the rest of your life?"

Another verbal slap in the face.

"You're an adult, Bri. Act like one."

I could only stare at her in shock. Nikki didn't spare another glance at me, instead turning and walking away. She slammed her car door and squealed her tires when she left the parking lot.

I sobbed so hard I collapsed to the ground. A few minutes later, Kevin pulled me into a huge hug. I wrapped my arms around his neck tight and cried.

"What a bitch," he said. "She could try to be more understanding."

"Thanks. You didn't need to come back outside." I hiccupped, unable to catch my breath. "Am I wrong for not telling Aidan I'm pregnant?"

"I refuse to touch that one."

I pulled away. "Kevin, be serious," I said, sniffing.

"Bri...I won't say if you are right or wrong," he said, sighing. He reached forward and wiped a few tears from my face. "No one can make your decisions for you. I'll give Nikki credit because she is right, you're an adult, but she had no right to talk to you that way."

"Nikki's not the bitch," I said, my voice cracking a bit. "I'm the horrible bitch for not telling him."

"Briana..." Kevin sighed and pulled my head to his chest, sitting in the middle of the parking lot with me. "I would want someone to tell me if I was going to be a dad. No one can tell you what to do. I don't even know what I'd do if..." He sucked in a deep breath and released it slowly. "I've never gotten far enough to think about having kids, but I think you're doing what you think is right for you and your son right now. I think that's the most important thing."

If he grew a beard one day, he would look exactly like our father. Listening to him talk in such a calming way reminded me of the way Dad used to hug us. He hugged me tighter and talked for a few minutes while I tried to calm down.

"Do you think we can get up now?" Kevin said. "People are looking at us weird."

I pulled back quickly, wiping my eyes.

"Sorry," I said, sniffing. "God, when did I turn into a drama queen?" I said, trying to pass off my total breakdown as a joke.

Kevin frowned at me. "That was the worst fight I ever saw you get into with one of your friends." He stood up and offered me a hand. I took it. "Come on. I'm hungry and we still need food."

"Um..." I said, grabbing his arm with my other hand when he helped me up. "Should we go somewhere else?"

An elderly lady stood near her minivan, arms crossed, as she scowled at me. Another woman held her daughter closer to her and walked past us quickly.

"I hate this town," Kevin grumbled. He threw an arm around my shoulder and walked with me back to the car. "We should definitely go somewhere else."

I jumped when my back pocket buzzed. I pulled out my phone. Lora was calling.

Thankfully I wasn't crying anymore.

"Hey. Where have you been?" I asked.

"I heard Kevin got in a fight today at school?" she said. Lora sounded upset, like she was trying to keep herself from freaking out but not managing to keep herself calm well. "Why didn't you tell me?"

"You disappeared on me. I had no idea where you were," I said. "I thought you were supposed to be at work."

Silence. I almost asked if she was still there but then I heard a bottle clink against something.

"I had somewhere to be," she said. "A doctor's appointment. I thought I told you?"

"Last time I checked, I was the one with the doctor's appointment," I hissed out. "Congratulations. You're going to be a great aunt to a little boy."

"Oh, don't remind me," Lora groaned, almost like she was in pain.

I gritted my teeth. She meant no harm. She probably got caught up last night and drank a little too much. She would be excited later eventually.

"Do I hear John's voice?"

"I usually take off work once a month for a checkup then come hang out at Rendezvous," she said. "I missed it the last couple times because we were trying to get you situated.

"Who is it?" Kevin mouthed.

"Lora," I mouthed back. His responded by rolling his eyes and taking my keys to open the doors. "Oh, okay," I said, returning to my phone and taking my keys back when he handed them to me. "Do you know when you'll be home?"

"Since it's a Friday I think I'm going to stay out late so don't wait up for me. You kids have some fun, okay?"

"All right," I said.

"Okay. I'll talk to you later."

"Wait, Lora," I said. "Don't go yet."

"Why?"

"You didn't tell Nikki I decided to stay in Tennessee? Why?"

"I figured you could use some time away from drama. You agreed at first not to tell her too."

"Yeah, well I just ran into her at the grocery store and she screamed at me in the parking lot."

"Oh, shit!" Lora said. "Oh, honey, are you okay?"

That's what it took for her to show concern?

I opened the car door and sat down, playing with my keys for a second before I answered her.

"No. It was awful. I can't—she yelled at me for not letting Aidan know I'm pregnant."

"Well...I'm not sure what to tell you, honey, other than you probably do need to tell him." We didn't say anything to each other for a few minutes, and I thought about hanging up the phone. "I'm glad you're having a little boy. I'm sorry, sweetie, I had a weird night. In fact, I'm so happy you're having a boy."

I sighed. "I'm not ready," I said. "I'm especially not ready after the reaction Nikki had. I wish I knew you didn't mention I stayed in Tennessee, and I needed some time to myself."

"I really don't have time for this right now," Lora said.

"What do you mean?" I asked, shocked.

"I'll see you kids later. I need to go."

I stared at my phone in shock when the call disconnected.

"Kevin...how long has Lora been drinking after work on Fridays?"

"Since you moved to college," he said. "She's been going out more."

"Do you think I need to worry about her?"

"I'm not sure," he said.

~*~

Aidan

I looked at the girl Cynthia finally talked me into going on a date with on Valentine's Day.

She was pretty; a classic kind of pretty. Her red hair stopped just along her jawline. She had legs that went on for miles in her green dress. She smelled like some sort of flowers. Kind of like Cynthia, actually. I wondered if she borrowed some of Cyn's perfume because she got ready at her apartment. She had a bright shade of red on her lips and enough eye makeup on to make her green eyes stand out.

I couldn't fucking believe my ex-girlfriend talked me into going on a date with a damn red head; at my favorite Italian place, no less. The same place I wanted to take Briana on a date to before she upped and disappeared on me.

No, I told myself. This was an attempt to move on. Cynthia figured out my attraction to redheads. Besides Briana wanted nothing to do with me so I would try to let it go. For now. I think Mom started to worry about me because I threw myself into working on the house and on the ranch so hard.

On top of this it was fucking Valentine's Day.

Little paper hearts and candies were all around.

"It smells good in here," she said when we took a seat.

"We have some of the best wine around," said the waiter. He placed the menus down in front of us. "Would you like anything?"

"Beer," I said.

"I'll have a glass of red? Surprise me, but I like sweeter wines."

"Ah," said the waiter. He nodded. "Good choice."

"And an antipasto platter," I added.

"What's that?"

Shit. I forgot her name.

Roll with it, I told myself.

"It's an appetizer," I said, "with meat and cheese."

"Oh," she said. "That's cool. But I'm—"

I wished I hadn't forgotten this girl's name.

She was easy to talk to. At some point during the conversation she scooted her chair closer to mine. She pushed her main dish—barely eaten chicken parmesan—forward and leaned to hold her head up with her hand so she could listen to me whenever I spoke. I was more interested in trying to get to know her. I learned she was at SU to get her biology degree like Cyn and that was how they met. She wanted to be a microbiologist. I think it meant more school or something. She seemed pretty down to earth—more down to earth than I originally thought when I met her.

"So you own horses," she said. "Do you breed them?"

"Mom does a little of everything on the ranch," I said. "Some of our horses have been in competitions."

"Oh," she said, leaning forward more. She placed her hand on my arm. "Like races?"

"A few of them are race horses, yeah."

"That's awesome. Cyn said you rescued a few horses, right?"

"Yeah," I said. "I ended up keeping my last rescue."

"Aww, what's its name?"

"Blue Moon. A stallion. When he came to us he was pretty wrecked. Last owner starved him and whipped him."

She gasped. "Poor baby."

"Yeah, he wasn't broke yet either. Was terrified of ropes. I don't know what I would've done without Briana. She was Cyn's roommate last semester. Her and Blue bonded instantly. Surprised the hell out of me because before that he didn't trust anyone, not even me, but she managed to get him to come around to being around ropes. First day I met her, she pointed that out to me, and I'd had Blue Moon for a while. The way she was able to get him to trust her was pretty amazing. She moved recently, didn't tell me why, and I think he misses her."

I continued to talk about Bri the rest of the night.

I *think* the date went pretty well.

Briana

Valentine's Day was overrated.

I focused on that instead of worrying if my aunt and her possible drinking problem.

I still helped Kevin pick out a card to give to Robin in the grocery store the day before. I shook my head as I stared at the sealed envelope on the kitchen table. As much as he wanted to give it to her he still hadn't had the guts to do it. He needed to soon if he wanted to let her know how he felt about her.

"I think he's hopeless," Lora said with a laugh as she flounced into the kitchen.

"He's going to a movie with her. Why doesn't he ever listen to me when I tell him the kind of stuff he can do to impress a girl? If he'd listen he would just—"

"No offense, honey, but you don't have the best track record with your love life."

I rolled my eyes. "Yeah, okay. At least I never saw my roommate's boyfriend's butt crack."

"Oh no," Lora said, mirth in her eyes. "But at least I didn't walk in on my roommate in the middle of getting heavy with her boyfriend's cousin on my brand new futon."

I made gagging sounds and pointed inside my mouth with my index finger. As much as I missed Cynthia, Lee, and Aidan, I didn't need the reminder. At least I was almost over morning sickness. That might have sent me to the toilet earlier in my pregnancy.

"Can I talk to you about something?" I asked, sitting down.

"Sure," Lora said.

"Do you have a problem with drinking?"

That thought kept plaguing me the whole entire night. I never thought my aunt would be the type to skip out on work or go spend a whole day drinking but she had. It worried me because right now she was the only thing keeping me and my brother afloat.

"No," Lora said, laughing. "Why would you think *that?*"

"It's just... you party a lot for a thirty-something."

Lora snorted. "What, you don't think I should party since I'm in my thirties?"

I shrugged, twisting my hair around my fingers. "It's just that Kev looks to you as a parental figure, and so do I. I...it worries me. If you're going to miss work and stuff sometimes I should get a job too. Can't the school fire you for missing a lot of work? I also can't help but feel like we're cramping your style or something."

"You're not cramping my style," Lora said. She poured herself a cup of coffee. "I think you should still try to go to school, and you need to consider adoption."

"Not an option."

I guess I spoke too soon when I said Lora stopped hounding me.

It seemed like that was my automatic response anymore. Lora wasn't satisfied if she mentioned adoption at least five times a day. She wanted me to go to college, and I wanted to finish my education too, but it was okay to put it on hold for a while, right? I thought so, anyway.

"Okay," Lora said. "It's fine. I make enough to keep you and your brother on your feet for a while."

"I kind of want a job, though," I said. "If I work for a while I'll be able to save some money and won't need to rely on student loans."

"You lost your grants, didn't you?"

I looked down. "Yeah."

Lora released a soft sigh. "You'll figure things out, Bri. You always do." She pulled her phone from her pocket. "Oh, crap, I need to do some Saturday school detention today so I need to get going."

"Okay," I said.

She gulped the rest of her coffee and grabbed her keys off the counter. Kissing me on the cheek, she pushed my hair out of my face, and stared down at me.

"Things will be okay. You need to stop worrying so much."

"Stop drinking so much. I'll worry less."

Lora rolled her eyes, waved, and left.

She would never listen. I shook my head and decided to have a Grey's Anatomy marathon on Netflix for the rest of the day.

Aidan

Blue Moon pressed his nose against my hand and blew hard. Neither one of us cared about the falling snow. I cared more that he had gotten into a burr bush and his hair was matted up into an unmanageable mess. If everyone didn't insist on keeping his mane long I would have taken scissors to it by now.

"Seriously, buddy?" I asked, setting the tack box on the ground.

I surveyed the damage he did this time. It wasn't just his mane got into a matted mess either, oh no. His whole tail was covered in burrs. First chance I got in the summer we were going to take care of those fucking weeds. Mom let them grow far too long.

"How in the hell do you even find any of these plants?"

Blue moon snorted softly and sniffed around my pockets.

"Sorry, boy," I said to him. "I don't have any sugar cubes."

He started to fill out nicely. Blue always stayed on the thin side until recently. I guess it was natural, since he had problems from neglect and starvation. His scar across his chest finally had a patch of fur growing back.

He snorted in protest.

"Okay, you got me."

I pulled a couple of sugar cubes in a baggy from my back pocket. Both of his ears shot forward and he sniffed loudly. He tried to take the bag but I laughed at him and pushed him away.

"Hold on sugar hog." I pulled the bag open, pulled out a sugar cube, then closed it back up and put it back in my pocket. I held my hand flat. "Here you go, boy."

"God, he got into the burrs again?"

I sighed. "Yeah."

Cyn walked up and rubbed Blue behind the ears. "He gets into so much trouble."

"Well, what am I going to do?" I shook my head. His whiskers tickled against my hand as he licked residual sugar from my palm. "I can't keep him boxed up in a stall. If I need to drop more money to fix mom's stables it might make me go broke."

She laughed. "You're so over dramatic sometimes."

I shrugged. "It is what it is."

"Speaking of, how did your date go?"

"She was a nice girl," I said. "I might take her again."

"She hates you."

My eyes widened. "What?"

"Paige hates you...like *literally* hates your guts. She said it was the worst date she's ever been on. What the *hell* did you do to her?"

Baffled, I shrugged and scratched the back of my head. "No idea. I thought things went well. I even kissed her at the end of the night."

"Aidan, she never wants to see you again. She said the antipasto was disgusting because she's vegan. She pushed her chicken parmesan away and you didn't notice how uncomfortable she was. You kept talking about Bri all night."

Oh. *That*. I forgot.

"Oh, uh..."

"Yeah, *uh*." She slapped my shoulder. "What the hell were you thinking!?"

"I was thinking it was my favorite Italian restaurant even though you set it up and it ain't my fault if she didn't tell me she's vegan!"

Cyn released a cry of frustration and threw her hands up in the air.

"You are impossible!"

"Well, I'm not ready to date," I said. "So quit trying to fix me up with your friends!"

"I shouldn't even need to worry, Aidan."

"Screw Peggy if she didn't like my date."

"*Paige!*" Cyn said. "It's Paige!"

"Whatever, Sinner."

Blue Moon snorted like he was laughing at us.

"Shut up," I muttered to my horse, patting his nose affectionately.

Cyn crossed her arms shook her head.

"What are we going to do with you?"

I ignored her, reaching down for a comb in the tack box.

"You're making everyone worry about you, Aidan."

Still said nothing. Maybe if I ignored her, she would go away. I was acting like a little bit of a five year old but what the hell did Cyn think would happen if she set me up on a date? I didn't know where the hell Briana was. To be fair to Paige, I *did act* bit of an ass. I talked about Bri. I forgot the girl's name. I tried to force to do something I didn't want to do and turned myself into a moron. But I didn't need Cyn to fucking remind me of the fact.

When she reminded me, it made me start thinking about how much I wished I'd been with Briana that night instead of one of Cyn's friends that I barely knew.

"God, if Aberlie didn't want to make me keep my mouth shut so much..."

If I hadn't been waiting for her to nag me some more I might have missed what she said, Cyn spoke in such a soft whisper. My eyes shot up to hers and I studied her, almost waiting for her to continue talking. Cyn turned a little red and stood straighter, backing away.

"You and Mom keeping something from me?"

Cyn shook her head. "No," she laughed. "Why would you think so?"

"Son of a bitch, *what* are you two keeping from me?"

There were hiding something and I refused going to let her laugh it off.

"It's nothing, Aidan."

"Cynthia, dammit!" I slammed the comb back down into the tack box. "I've been killing myself wondering what the hell happened, what I did wrong to make Briana leave. If you know something, if you can tell me anything, tell so I can stop killing myself over it!"

Blue whinnied in protest and stepped away from me.

"It's nothing, seriously!"

She walked away from me more confused than ever.

Briana

I dropped my purse on the floor.

"You've got to be *fucking* kidding me," I said, looking up at the ceiling and throwing up my hands.

I picked up the papers on my bed.

They were pamphlets. Adoption pamphlets. Things about closed versus open adoption, names of agencies, why it was a good idea to give the baby up for adoption if you felt you weren't ready to be a parent yet. Lora couldn't be happy about my baby boy. No, instead, she had to not so subtly suggest I give him up so I could keep going to college.

I stomped into the living room where John and Lora sat watching a movie, pamphlets in hand.

"What the hell is this?" I asked.

Lora turned quickly. John lazily looked at me, a drink in his hand. I tossed the adoption pamphlet at my aunt.

"Oh, I thought you might want to see them."

I threw my hands up in the air. "I've gone over this with you like *ten* times now, Lora. I'm not giving him up for adoption."

"You know, me and Lora were talking about this earlier—"

"Excuse me, John, if I don't really give a damn about your opinions since I don't know you."

That was it.

She would either answer me or she wouldn't I needed Nikki. .I wasn't sure what to do. I didn't even care if she had my new number.

The first time she didn't pick up. It went straight to voicemail.

I collapsed on my bed after I hit "end" on the phone.

And redialed her number.

Voice mail again. I'd seen her spring semester schedule because I was there when she was picking out classes. I didn't think she was in class. I still had her email about her work schedule. I grabbed my laptop off my pillow and looked at it. She wasn't at work.

So, I called her a third time, and shoved the stupid pamphlets under my bed with my foot as far as I could get them.

"Are you going to call me like fifty million times?"

"Yeah," I said, nearly sobbing in relief. "I am. I need you."

"Yeah, well, you have a funny way of showing it."

She started to say something else but I cut her off.

"I'm fucking terrified, Nikki."

"You're pregnant, not about to die of cancer. What is there to be scared of?"

"You're seriously asking me that question?"

"...Yeah, I think I am."

"Kevin isn't out of school. I'm supposed to be in college right now. Do you think I can go to school and raise a baby? I'm not even sure if Aidan is ready to be a father! He's too wrapped up in his ranch."

"You know what? You are right. If you can run away and not tell me you didn't run back to Kentucky then maybe you aren't ready to be a mother. Lora told me she's been trying to get you to give the baby up for adoption."

"Everyone seems to think that's the best option right now."

"Yeah. Maybe it would be."

"It's not happening. I refuse. I can't give up a part of myself. I can't abandon this baby."

Nikki sighed. I could hear it in her voice—she felt defeated. She was as tired of fighting with me as I with her.

"Nikki... I need you right now. I need my *best* friend. I don't think I can do this without you having my back. Please tell me you have my back? I'm sorry I lied about moving. I just... I needed time away from everything."

"I'm mad at you." Her voice sounded shaky.

"I realize that. I really do. But please...don't punish me for not being upfront with you. I needed to leave, and I did. I fully intended on staying in Kentucky but Lora wouldn't let me and now she keeps insisting on this adoption thing and... Running would be easier."

"Don't you dare!"

"I'm not going to... I might want to but I can't. Kevin needs me."

Nikki released a huge sigh of relief.

"Good. I need you to have my back too... I slept with Lee."

I sat up so fast my head span.

"You did what!?"

"Yeah... I slept with Lee."

"Lee like Aidan's cousin, Lee?"

"Yeah, that one."

"What the *hell* is wrong with you?"

"I got mad at you...then Cynthia and Aidan because if they hadn't dragged you into their open relationship shit then you wouldn't have gotten pregnant. We wouldn't have ever gotten into a stupid fight. I still talk to Lee even though you've tried your hardest to keep yourself away from everyone. We had a couple drinks at The Roadhouse. Next thing I know I've had one too many shots of whiskey and coke and I'm waking up in my bedroom with this big, gorgeous guy next to me."

"Does Cynthia know?"

I could see her shaking her head. Cynthia didn't know. Oh, man, this was so messed up. My heart actually felt like it wanted to break for Cyn. She didn't deserve for this to happen.

"Stupid, Nikki. STUPID."

"I know that! The worst part is he's engaged to her and he hasn't talked to me since it happened."

"Wait, hold up, they're engaged!?"

"Briana, tell Aidan you're pregnant. You're missing on way too much stuff going on over here."

"I'm not ready. I'm still processing—you slept with Lee and he's engaged to Cynthia!?"

"Yes! Okay? I was stupid!"

"Because you got mad at me!?"

"Well, I'm pretty sure the alcohol had something to do with it."

I raked my hand through my hair. I honestly didn't know what to say to her. Words wouldn't form no matter how much I tried to get something out. I tried for the past few days to get my mind off what happened, and suddenly, I was pulled right back into the drama. I wondered if not moving back to Kentucky was an honest mistake—maybe I should have stood my ground, but instead I was living with my aunt, who couldn't seem to understand that I would be keeping this baby no matter how many times she wanted to suggest I do otherwise. I worried about her drinking too much. My brother fought with other boys to defend his girlfriend's honor. My best friend slept with my ex-roommate's fiancé.

I wasn't sure what Aidan was up to.
I didn't know if I wanted to.

"Oh, and don't worry... Aidan is pretty much still moping over you."

"I can't say I care about him. You're stupid."

"Lee told me Cyn talked him into a date with a potential maid of honor and all he did was talk about you."

"Aidan is stupid too."

"I miss you. Can I come over sometime?"

"I can't believe he's going on a date. What's her name?"

"I think it started with a 'P'? I can't remember but apparently Cynthia got super excited. I know she's a redhead."

"I'm going to—" For the first time in a while, I felt nauseous. "I'll call you back later."

I didn't throw up.

But I also didn't expect to hear what I heard. Everything sounded like it was crazy over there. What was wrong with everyone?

I didn't call Nikki back. Not at first, anyway. I couldn't bring myself to. It hurt me more than I realized to hear Cyn talked Aidan into going on a date. It wasn't fair to me... even though logically, I knew I left, and he had every right to be mad. He could try to move on with his life. I guess the date didn't work out for him in the end, but I needed to know what was what was going on in his life.

I made up my mind. I needed to tell him... but I wasn't sure how I would do it.

I also would not be giving my son up for adoption. Lora could try as much as she wanted to but it wouldn't happen. If she tried again, she would learn quickly that it was not her decision. I even started to wonder if I needed to move out and get my own place with Kevin.

Maybe I overthought the drinking thing. She only did it a couple nights a week with John, who recently became her boyfriend. Lora and I always tried to stay close because we were close in age. Sometimes she acted like my sister rather than my aunt, and I was protective over her. But, bottom line, she was an adult. I couldn't tell her to stop drinking any more than she could tell me to give my baby up for adoption.

It was time I did what Nikki told me I needed to do the day we saw each other in the grocery store parking lot.

I needed to pull up my big girl panties and stop acting like a scared little girl.

Chapter Seven

Aidan

"What do you mean, you need us to wait a year to get married?"

Lee halted in his tracks, chips crunching in his mouth as he bit down. Mom sat on the couch with a pile of yarn in her lap. She had a couple baby blankets or something to make for her church. I figured I would hang around for a few hours and bullshit with my cousin since he was helping me remodel my house.

Cynthia chewed my ass out and made me feel like an inconsiderate jerk to the girl I took on a date because I did nothing but talk about Briana with her.

I needed to rethink my life.

Getting my house finished was my top priority, as well as trying to get closer to my cousin. Lee wanted me to be his best man even though I never expected him to because Cynthia and I used to date. It was a vague memory by now; Cynthia and Lee deserved to be happy with each other.

I snorted. "Sorry, brother," I said, clapping Lee on the back when he glanced at me, his eyes pleading to get him out of this situation. "You're on your own." I grabbed the chips out of his hand and shoved a handful in my mouth. It was flavored with salt and vinegar. It tasted like shit, but neither one of us could ever stop eating them.

"Dick."

"Language," Mom said. "I'm knitting for a church event."

"I know," I said to Lee. "And Mom, you seriously think anyone is going to want a giant orange blanket?"

I ducked the couch pillow that flew at my head.

"Baby, I thought we talked about this last night?" Lee said, turning his attention to his fiancée. "We need to set the wedding sometime next year. Didn't you think June would be a good time?"

"What if I don't *want* to wait a year?" Cynthia would be in a full on whine-and-be-heard mode until she got her way. I knew this move well. She used to bitch and nag she got what she wanted from me. Feeling bad for Lee wasn't an option; he brought this on himself for being stupid in thinking he could get away with trying to ask her to reschedule the wedding. "I never asked you if you wanted to change your mind about the wedding plans... you sprung it up on me that you don't want to get married yet!"

I burst out laughing and sat next to mom, hugging the pillow she gave to me. I don't think either one of us expected this to happen when he told Cynthia he didn't want to get married this May.

I knew they talked about May only because Cynthia wouldn't stop gushing about it the day he agreed to it.

"Oh Aidan," Mom said in a teasing tone, "Don't provoke her. A bride planning her wedding is a dangerous creature."

Cynthia glared at us but turned her attention back to Lee. "I don't see a reason we need to wait. It's stupid. We love each other. Why do we need to wait?

Lee laughed, almost like he couldn't believe he was having this conversation with her in front of us.

"Maybe because I'm not ready to get married yet? We're engaged, Cyn. We need to take things one step at a time, not all at once in one giant leap."

"But Dad already refused to pay for the wedding and if we wait he might turn family against me and then no one will show up and—"

She sounded panicky.

"Hey, Sinner," I said.

She snapped her hateful, I-Want-To-Kill-You look at me; the one that usually meant I got to sleep on the couch while we were still together. I no longer had to live under that threat so I chuckled at the immediate way it caught her attention. "Breathe, princess," I said.

I'm lucky she doesn't have the ability to set humans on fire with those big brown eyes.

"Listen, Cynthia, a year or we aren't—"

I cleared my throat loudly to stop Lee from saying something stupid.

"Okay," Mom said, putting her knitting down. "I had no idea your father refused to pay for the wedding."

I smirked and crossed my arms.

"Yeah," Cyn said. "He's refusing."

She growled and threw a pillow at me because, despite myself, I burst out laughing again.

"You look like you're about to make poor Lee pass out," Mom said. "Why don't I just pay for the wedding? You're like a daughter anyway."

"Aww, Aberlie, you don't need to," Lee said.

Despite all her griping about Cynthia to my father, and to myself, Mom loved Cynthia. She undeniably became a part of the family through the years.

Cynthia stared at her phone. "I—I guess that would be okay." She walked over to Lee, heels clicking loudly on the ground. She kissed him on the cheek. "I need to get going since Bobby needs me to cover a later shift."

"Cyn, are you okay, baby?" Lee asked.

She wasn't okay.

Lee and I looked at each other. Shit. There wasn't much we could do, however, because Cynthia turned right back around to leave.

"What am I going to do with you boys?" Mom asked, rolling her eyes before resumed knitting.

~*~

I realized a few days after Cyn and Lee's argument that I was lonely.

I wanted to find Briana.

I couldn't focus on that. Instead, I threw myself into working on the house. I didn't have control over whether or not Briana contacted me, but I did have control over what kind of condition my house was in. Cyn and Lee decided they did want to move into my apartment as a test run for their marriage. I figured it was a good idea, and I couldn't leave my lease without a big fat fee of five hundred dollars for terminating early.

I found molded carpet under a crumbling built-in bookshelf in the living room a few weeks ago. The mold traveled up all the way to the ceiling so I needed to rip all of that out before someone could take care of the mold the best they could. Decay was normal in a house as old as mine, but if the tenants had taken better care of it, and there hadn't been a break in, the issues wouldn't have been nearly as bad. Now it was mid-March, and most of the mold problem had been eliminated.

"What the hell does 'Shangri La' have to do with purple paint?" Lee asked, staring at the paint samples in front of us.

Bobby scratched his head. "Huh? That isn't even the worst one. What the fuck is Embricardo and how is it a color?"

"Who names this shit?" I asked, just as puzzled as my cousin and my best friend. "Why the hell can't blue just be blue and red just be red?"

"Remind me why you have to paint your house again?" Bobby asked. "Why don't you just slap some kind of wall paper on it and call it a done day?"

I frowned at him.

"Wall paper is tacky."

I couldn't believe I just fucking said that, or that we were having this conversation.

I wish Mom could do this shit.

"It'd still be a lot easier than choosing paint colors... unless you want to go with something like... Chocolate Froth."

I raised an eyebrow and looked at the paint sample he pointed out to me.

It was fucking white paint.

"Aunt Abs will have his hide, that's why. She said to make it look bright."

"She isn't going to be living in it so I don't know why it matters," I said, shaking my head. I grabbed a pile of paint samples. "Whatever. I'm just going to give them to Mom and let her choose."

"We should've just asked Cyn to come," Lee said.

"I'm giving you my apartment. I'm not letting Cyn touch these because shit like Chocolate Froth will end up on my walls."

"Abs isn't any better," Lee said.

"She'll still ask me before she gets the paint. Cyn will decide to get artistic on it with her friends or some bullshit and I'm not willing to let that happen."

Lee chuckled under his breath. "Actually if I let anyone paint the apartment I think I might ask Nikki to."

That made me freeze in my tracks.

"Nikki? Seriously?"

"The girl has a crazy brain but she's artistic as hell. She could do the math on how much I'd need to spend for the paint and then make it look amazing."

"I didn't know you were still spending time with her."

"Yeah," Lee said, shrugging.

"Cynthia know about that, man?" Bobby asked.

"Yeah. She knows we like to hang out sometimes. She tells me its fine. Cynthia is really cool like that. She doesn't get jealous."

Cynthia used to bitch about how oblivious I could act when we dated.

I almost said something to him, but I just didn't know how to put what I wanted to say into words. Something rolled over me—anger, I think—because he was talking to Nikki. Had they talked about Briana? Did Lee maybe know more about where she was than I did?

Fuck that noise.

I wasn't going to worry about it. They were friends. Good. Lee needed more friends. I wouldn't insult Nikki because she wanted to protect her friend, but Cynthia needed better girlfriends. I'd told her that a long time ago and she never wanted to listen to me. Maybe if Lee and Nikki spent enough time together, Cyn might start wanting to spend time with her too. I knew from the fact that Cyn told Lee it was "fine" for him to spend time with Nikki that she might not be so fine with it but Cynthia was really a cool chick. She hadn't ever gotten jealous if I spent time with other female friends even though I didn't have many of them.

So, instead of saying anything, I kept my mouth shut and went back to looking at paint samples. I focused on the stupid ass names and tried to decide what shade would go best in my living room even though I really didn't give a rat's ass what shade of blue went in my house.

I looked in the cart where I threw the paint samples. I had other things in there like paint tape and new outlet covers for the wall. I had to replace a few lights too so I had an assortment of other things in the cart. Since I'd be living on the ranch and would still be working for mom she offered to help me pay for mostly everything I was doing to the house and I gladly took the help. Remodeling got expensive real quick.

"So uh..." Bobby said, him and Lee slowly walking next to me when I decided I had everything I needed paint-sample wise and pushed the cart out of the aisle. "How are you doing?"

"What do you mean?" I asked.

Lee and Bobby looked at each other. I raised an eyebrow but kept walking, not sure if I wanted to know what those two were thinking.

"I mean since Briana left. How are you doing?"

I should've figured that's what he was going to ask me. I'd been trying for the past month to forget about her. She didn't want to be found, I wasn't going to try to find her. I wasn't going to keep harassing her best friend to let me know where she moved.

"I'm doing fine," I said.

"I don't know, man," Lee said. "It seems like you're trying to do things to keep yourself busy. Did you really have to clean out the other barn by yourself yesterday?"

"So what if I'm keeping myself busy?" I asked. "I like being busy. If I want to be busy, I'll stay busy."

"Do you seriously need to replace all the lights in the house?" Bobby asked.

"Get to the point," I said. "Why are you guys bringing this up now? Do I need to remind you that I'm trying to get out of my apartment as fast as I can so that you can move into my apartment, Lee?"

"Yeah," he said, "I know that you're trying to get out of there as soon as possible. But it's the other shit you're doing that is starting to make Cyn and Aunt Abs worry about you."

I snorted. "Sure, if those two were worried about me, they'd say something."

"Look, maybe I could find you someone other than one of Cyn's friends to date. Someone who might be more understanding. There's this really hot blonde chick who is friends with Sam—"

"Fuck that, Bobby. I'm happy being single."

Chapter Eight

Briana

I wrung my hands together, completely nervous.

Nikki told me she wanted to come over, so I told her to. It only took us until I was thirty weeks pregnant for her to finally admit she wanted to forgive me, and for I to admit I missed her.

I didn't know all of the details of her affair with Lee, and I wasn't sure if I wanted to. It felt...wrong, prying into my best friend's life. A while ago I might not have had an issue but the more I thought about it, the more I didn't want to know all the sordid details. Knowing them meant another one of my friends would be hurt when she found out, and even though I wasn't talking to Cynthia right now, I would eventually. I couldn't stand the thought of her finding out I knew something so life changing about her relationship with Lee and I didn't let her know. It didn't matter that Cynthia didn't have my new number or that she had no idea where I was right now. She would find out...as soon as I got up the guts to let Aidan know I was now thirty weeks pregnant

I had no idea where Lora was but she gave me some crap about needing to do some extra work at the school. She said would give Kevin and Robin a ride home. I guess she had a lot of test papers to grade or something? It didn't matter. The good thing is that Nikki wouldn't need to listen to her rant at me about needing to give the baby up for adoption.

"I'm so freaking glad you called me!"

Nikki launched herself at me, pulling me into a huge hug. She had at least four bags on her left arm that hit my back but I didn't care, as happy to see her as she was to see me. I hugged her tightly; the stupid urge to start sobbing came hard and fast.

"I am too," I said. "I didn't realize how bad I actually needed a girl's night!"

"You're telling me," Nikki said, pulling away. She walked into the living room, not missing a beat while she talked. "I needed to talk to you about so many things I can't even begin to count them on one hand."

"I thought we were going to watch a few movies," I said, laughing. "I didn't know you were going to bring other things."

"Oh, this?" she held up the bags.

My eyes went wide. "You did not go shopping for my son!"

"Of course I did," Nikki said. "You're so focused on avoiding Aidan and whatever other crap that is going, I don't think you stopped to actually *enjoy* the fact you have a baby on the way. Have you even looked at cribs yet?"

She handed me the bag, from a local baby store I'd stared at a while but never had the guts to go into.

"You didn't need to do this," I said. "Baby clothes?"

"Yeah. I hope all the blue is okay..."

"Nikki, you're amazing."

I took a seat on the couch and rifled through the first bag. T-shirts, onesies, bibs. Nikki went all out, having spent more than she probably had for my son. Lora hadn't even offered to help me get a crib yet.

A big fat tear rolled down my face.

"You really didn't have to do this."

"Well, I wanted to," she said. "I'm mad at you for disappearing like you did, but that doesn't mean I don't love you or what to be your little guy's aunt."

"Seriously?"

I burst out laughing. The shirt I pulled from the bag had six baby bottles on it, and said, "Check out my six pack."

"I couldn't resist."

"You're terrible," I said, giggling.

She wrapped her arms around me again in a tight hug.

"Don't get all blubbery on me. I have the first season of *Angel!* You can blubber as much as you want to when they have the *Buffy* crossover!"

I didn't know where Lora and Kevin were.

It was almost nine at night.

She was supposed to bring him home from school after Nikki left. I started seriously worrying about them both around seven. I'd texted and called Lora several times to try to get her to talk to me. Kevin's phone kept going right to voice mail. I couldn't figure out why. On top of all of this my back was hurting and I felt like I had a bad case of gas.

There was only one place I could think of that Lora would take Kevin. I wondered if Robin was with them too because Lora said she would give her a ride home. I really didn't want it to be Rendezvous. It was a Friday night. It was a restaurant, after all. But after eight at night livened up, with a live band and a lot of alcohol. Thus far Lora hadn't ever kept him too late.

I was pretty sure that's what happened.

"This is ridiculous," I said to myself in a huff. I spent five minutes looking for my flats—oh, how I grew to *hate* putting on tennis shoes the past few weeks because I now had to struggle a little to get them tied—and my keys and my purse. Of course, I never kept everything in one place, so it took me about fifteen minutes to find everything I needed.

Purse, check. Flats and decent looking yoga pants, check. I recently started making a mental list of everything so I would forget nothing. Sometimes I could be pretty forgetful, but lately, it was like I couldn't remember anything unless I created a mental checklist. I almost forgot I had to get Kevin from school so that's when Lora told me she would start picking him up for me on Fridays so I could focus on other things like looking into online programs so I could finish my English degree.

I'd decided I would finish school. It would take longer, and I didn't like being in a large university classroom anyway.

"Nikki," I said after I opened the front door, "what are you doing here?"

She crossed her arms. "Sorry if it's not a good time. I can leave."

She turned but I reached for her hand.

"No, I'm sorry," I said. "I just didn't expect you to come over. I thought we weren't going to hang out until next weekend?"

"Well I might have mentioned you're pregnant to Lee..."

"You what?" I asked, panic burrowing its way into my belly. The baby kicked I smoothed a hand over my belly to calm him. "Oh my god, Nikki! What is wrong with you? I thought you agreed with my decision to not let anyone know. You gave me baby clothes!"

"I realize that," Nikki said. "But there is a lot on my plate right now. I'm sleeping with an engaged man and my best friend is pregnant with his cousin's baby! What do you *expect* me to do? I crack under stress!"

"You do not understand the meaning of stress right now," I started.

"You weren't lying, baby. Fuck."

My eyes snapped to Lee's, and then down to my stomach. I glared at Nikki.

"Why the hell doesn't Aidan know?"

I dug my keys out of my pocket and stepped outside. I drew in a deep breath. I wasn't prepared for this. I wanted to know where my aunt and brother were. That was my top priority. I didn't even wait for Nikki to back up when I shut the door and locked it.

"I don't have time for this right now," I said. "I realize you're probably mad at me."

"A little bit, yeah," Lee said.

"I think Aidan needs to know. It killed me not telling Lee. I can't imagine what Aidan will think when he finds out," Nikki said.

"Look, it's my decision to make. You have to admit that Aidan and Cyn weren't the most honest with me about everything that went on in their relationship."

Cyn's abortion, of course. Maybe I felt a little self-righteous because I wanted to keep my own baby. I ran my hand across my stomach to soothe the both of us at the thought.

"What are you talkin' about, Briana? Aidan is fucking killing himself trying to forget about you," Lee said.

Shut it out, I told myself. You're pregnant. You don't need this right now.

In an attempt to try to ignore him I brushed past both Nikki and Lee, not giving them another thought. Maybe they would get the message. How dare she spring this on me when I told her earlier that I wasn't ready to tell anyone yet? I didn't want to be stressed out. I didn't want Aidan to know about the baby. If anything, I thought Nikki would try to respect my wishes.

"He's been throwing himself into bullshit busywork to try to forget about you. You left for no reason. Hell, I think you even hurt Cynthia a little."

I whipped around. "That's a little hypocritical, don't you think?"

Nikki knew exactly what I meant. She looked down and idly messed with her hair.

"What do you mean?" Lee asked.

Typical male. They never realized they were doing something wrong until it was too late.

"Don't you think it's kind of shitty? You're cheating on Cynthia but telling me I hurt her? I'm correct when I guess you haven't said a *damn* thing about messing around with Nikki, *right?*"

"That's none of your business."

"Oh, Lee," I laughed. "You're so wrong when you tell me it's none of my business. Someone's heart is going to get broken. It always happens when three people are involved in a relationship. At least Aidan had the decency to be open about his feelings for me and Cynthia during the whole open relationship mess. I'm pretty sure Cyn has no idea." I opened my door. "Oh, and if you let Lee tell Aidan about my pregnancy, I'm never speaking to you again, Nikki. I'll tell him when I'm ready."

I sat down in my car, the blood rushing to my brain. I couldn't believe I spoke to them both like that. At least I could blame it on hormones and stress? I had no desire to be in a big confrontation in the middle of the night, and that's what it would have turned into had I stayed.

I slammed my car door, angry, unable to believe Nikki actually brought Lee to the house when I specifically asked her not to. I was not easy on my car when I tore out of the driveway.

Aidan

Fresh from a shower, I walked out of my bathroom. I expected Bobby to call me any minute because the two of us decided to go get a few drinks. We hadn't lately. Working on the house kept me busy and working at his clinic kept him busy. He had to find a new receptionist because his old one upped and quit on him. Cynthia refused to do any basic work since she almost had her degree so he kept getting frustrated with her.

The two of us needed a hard, stiff drink, and to spend time away from everyone. Apparently Samantha got pissed at Bobby earlier because he didn't want to get married yet. I don't know. Something about women, one of them gets engaged, all of a sudden they all want to start settling down. I invited Lee to come with us too but he said he had other plans.

"Aidan, are you home?" Mom asked.

I glanced down.

Buck naked.

Shit.

"Hey Mom," I yelled back to her.

"I got you some groceries!"

I grabbed my phone. Lee sent me a few messages, and I missed a call from Bobby. Double shit. It was also nine thirty.

"Hold on! Just got out of the shower, I'll be out in a minute."

"Okay, sweetie. I'll put away your..."

Fuck. I guess Mom noticed the mess in my kitchen. So what if I let a few dishes pile up? And left clothes on the couch. And had random stuff packed in a half-assed manner.

I got dressed quickly, deciding it wasn't safe to leave her out there for long. Mom hated messes. She yelled at me a few times when I was a teenager and refused to clean my room, and she wasn't above doing the same thing now.

"Aidan McCoy," she said as soon as I walked out of my room, a hand on her hip. "What the hell is this?"

Yep. My messy apartment pissed Mom off.

"Uh..." I stammered, glancing around.

For the first time in a while I felt truly embarrassed. Mom usually bought my groceries but the past few times I had her give me the money so I could get what I needed on my own.

I'm grown man.

I shouldn't need to rely on my mother to grocery shop for me.

"I've been busy."

"Aidan, that's not an excuse. I'm just busy as you are."

"The dishwasher broke."

Mom raised an eyebrow, closed my messy dishwasher, and turned it on.

"It seems like it works fine to me."

"Shit, Mom, I'm just busy."

"The house is almost finished. You could take care of yourself a little more."

"If that's all you came here for other than to get me groceries—and thanks—you should leave."

"All right, what's wrong? You have been in a funk for months and I thought taking off with your father to go on a drinking binge was the height of it. Obviously, I'm wrong."

I ran my right hand through my wet hair and grumbled under my breath.

"Sorry, what, son?"

"I don't want to talk about it."

"Well you should still talk about it because I happened to find this weird ad online. Apparently Blue Moon is still for sale."

Fuck.

"So what if I want to sell my horse?"

"I can't believe you are even still considering it!" She yelled, slamming her hand on the counter. Dishes rattled in the sink and a grocery bag fell to the ground. "He's a rescue! I swore a long time ago I would *never* sell a rescue horse, and if you're going to work for my ranch I expect you to follow the same principle!"

"A rule I think is pretty stupid if you ask me. I'm charging an adoption fee."

"You're not getting rid of him," Mom said, firmly. "If you do, you're fired."

I glared at her. "You can't."

"You think I can't? Lee expressed interest in taking over the ranch. You're my baby boy, and I love you, but I will be damned if I let you get rid of Blue Moon. Lee might be my nephew but he's like a second son. You love Blue Moon. You're only mad because of one little accident because your girlfriend left without a word."

"Briana wasn't ever my girlfriend."

"If she wasn't your girlfriend, why the hell are you acting like such a pissy cry baby about it?"

"What the hell does that mean, Mom?"

Needing something to do, I pushed past her and grabbed the bag of cans.

"If Briana meant so little to you, you need to get the fuck over it already. I understand you're trying to become more independent by moving into your house, but only so much will help until you grow some balls." She huffed and snatched the bag of cans from me.

"Mom, with all due respect, get the hell out of my apartment."

Mom slammed the cans into the sink. "She took a pregnancy test."

My heart slammed against my rib cage.

"What?"

"You heard me. Briana took a pregnancy test."

"You're just saying that to fuck with me."

"I am not fucking with you. Dog food made her sick. Cyn and I had her take a test."

My head spun. I leaned against my fridge and ran my hand over my face and through my wet hair. No way did Briana take a test. She was pregnant. Sure, she hadn't felt good. She got sick the night before but she was fine the next morning.

Wait.

She was sick before she left.

"Shit."

"Exactly," Mom said.

"Do you know what the results were?"

"No, but she left right after she took it. I don't think it takes much to figure out what happened there, son."

"Fuck," I said. "I need to find her."

"I have a good feeling she's still at her aunt's but neither one of them want anyone to know."

"Lora threatened to call the cops on me if I go back over there."

"Fuck her aunt. I'll go over with you if you need me to."

"Mom, if Briana is staying there, that means she's scared to tell me. Why the hell would she be scared to tell me?"

Mom released a heavy sigh. "That's the million dollar question, isn't it, son?"

Briana

It took everything not to dissolve into an uncontrollable mess.

Seeing Lee brought back everything when I mostly tried to forget everything about Aidan. I almost managed it. I decided it would be better to try to move on with my life rather than to dwell on the past even though I knew I needed to talk to him eventually. Nikki and I were almost on the right track to becoming friends again. She'd gotten me baby clothes for my son. We laughed and cried during one of the most heartbreaking episodes in *Angel*. She painted my toes for me since it was hard to do now over my growing belly... but then she brought her new gentleman caller to see me.

I had to lay off the Jane Austen novels. I rolled my eyes at the thought. *Gentleman caller*. What was this? The eighteenth century? I loved Nikki. I did. I didn't agree with her ability to overlook the fact that she was having sex with another woman's fiancé. She also apparently couldn't care less about what private information she shared, too.

Deep breaths.

I had to keep reminding myself to take deep breaths.

I became emotional more lately. It had to be the pregnancy hormones. I'd read more about pregnancy and lurked on pregnancy forums on the internet and realized a lot of what I was feeling was normal. Add to the fact that I was not in a healthy relationship with the baby's father; more stress abound. Lora possibly taking off to a bar with my brother on a Friday night did not help matters either.

More deep breaths.

I didn't think it was appropriate for Lora to take Kevin there though.

The urge to cry turned into complete anger when I found Lora's car in the Rendezvous parking lot.

I was right.

I couldn't believe her.

What gave her the right?

I slammed my breaks on in front of the restaurant, giving zero fucks about parking properly.

In and out with my brother; that was the goal. I couldn't stay long. I heard the live band through the doors before I even opened the door.

"I'm sorry, there's a wait—"

I whipped around. I didn't care who the hostess was or if she needed to seat people. I wanted my brother out of here.

"I'm not staying."

"Well, I can't let you go inside unless you're going to have a seat at the bar...and if you ask me, that's really a bad idea for you."

I crossed my arms. This girl was young, and blonde. She wasn't really any older than me but as pissed off as I was I couldn't believe she would make assumptions.

"Siobhan, right?" I asked.

She looked down at her name tag and then me in confusion. "Yeah..."

"Okay, awesome. I'll let John know you're an idiot. I'm here to pick up my brother. His girlfriend is my aunt."

She gasped and tried to say something to defend herself but I didn't care.

Sure enough, I saw Kevin sitting next to Lora and John. He looked completely bored, and like he'd tried to start homework but he couldn't, and was instead trying to listen to the band. Robin sat next to him, just as uninterested.

"Lora, what the hell is going on?" I asked, yelling over the music.

Lora almost choked on her beer.

"Briana! What are you doing here?"

"Should I be asking you that?" I said, taking her beer from her. "You brought my brother and his girlfriend to a bar? What the *hell* is wrong with you!?"

I glared at her. John stood up and tried to take her beer back but I glared back at him, so angry I almost couldn't see straight. He pulled hard on the beer and I finally let go, scoffing and wiping my hand on my jeans when some of it spilled onto my fingers.

"I'll be right back," Lora said, sighing heavily. "We need to talk, Briana."

"Damn right we do!" I yelled, near tears. "Kids, go get in the car."

"Thank god," Kevin said, looking up at the ceiling. He stood and grabbed Robin's hands. "I'm sorry I didn't let you know what was going on. I left my phone in my locker."

"I'm not cool enough to have a phone," Robin added.

Lora dragged me in the other direction but not before I shoved my keys into my brother's hands. I'd never wanted to hit someone in my family so bad before. I legitimately wanted to hit her. Maybe even punch her, and I hadn't ever punched someone before even though sometimes Cynthia deserved it for the way she acted when I finally started dating Aidan.

"What is wrong with you?" I said, not giving Lora a chance to try to calm me down.

"This isn't just a bar, Bri," Lora said, almost laughing a little. She was drunk. I couldn't believe she was drunk while Kevin and Robin were with her. "It's a restaurant too."

"You're drunk. What would keep someone from calling the cops because you're drinking and you have minors with you? What's to say it wouldn't cause such a major problem that Robin's parents would forbid her from dating Kevin?"

"*God*," Lora said, "pregnancy hormones have turned you into a bitch. Relax. This is also a family restaurant."

I wanted to slap her.

Instead I decided to take her keys. She struggled, trying to push me off, shrieking and screaming for John when I forced her against a wall near the woman's bathroom and grabbed her keys from her back pocket.

He didn't come. I doubt he could hear her through the music. She was too drunk to fight me properly and as I dangled the keys in front of her and snapped them behind my back, I was thankful she wasn't more coherent because it could have hurt the baby.

"Come home when, and *only* when, you're sober."

Chapter Nine

Briana

Almost two weeks later I still hadn't spoken to Lora. She decided to stay with John for the time being, I supposed. I didn't know whether to call her or just ignore it.

I thought *she* was supposed to be an adult?

If anything, I should have been the one sneaking my brother out to see live music with his girlfriend.

I rolled my eyes and put my phone on the coffee table. Who was I kidding? I felt too responsible for Kevin and Robin to do something so reckless.

"You'll try putting me through this in about

sixteen or seventeen years," I said to my tummy. "Guess what, kid? There's nothing Mommy hasn't done that you'll be able to get away with... and stay out of open relationships. Those things are *messy.*"

I'd been reading up on fetal development recently. He could hear me. He had strong, solid kicks and loved to listen to my voice. I didn't want to be the type of mother who automatically went into baby voice mode whenever she spoke to her kid. I tried to speak to him like he was a little person... a little person who would depend on me for the next eighteen years.

The stupid baby voice still came out sometimes.

"Stop kicking so much, baby," I said. "Mommy wants to keep her orange juice down."

Anger couldn't describe how I felt. I spent a lot of the time by myself, especially on the weekends. Kevin begged me to let him spend Saturday night and most of Sunday at Robin's house. Apparently she had a brother, and both boys hit it off, and neither he nor Robin wanted to exclude her brother because he would be going into the army after he graduated high school in June.

How could I say no to that?

After a very uncomfortable and reassuring conversation with Robin's father, I gave in and let Kevin go over there. I sort of felt like a selfish child myself. Time to myself would be a rare thing in just a few short months. Lora's refusal to check in and let me know she was okay, and Kevin's weekend with Robin and her family, was a small blessing in disguise. My uncontrollable urge to clean, sore back, and swollen feet served as a stark reminder that I had a healthy baby.

The house looked like it had five teenagers living in it rather than one. Lora tried but she didn't know how to keep her place clean. She made half assed attempts to straighten up before she usually gave up and called John to see if he wanted to spend time together. In fact I think she was busier dating her boyfriend than grading her students. She barely had time to stop and throw a few dishes in the dishwasher and I was getting sick of it. Kevin didn't help at all either.

He loved to leave his backpack on the couch.

I tried to pick it up and gave up in two seconds.

"Geez," I said, rubbing my back and huffing. "Uncle Kevin keeps boulders in his backpack, doesn't he, sweetie?"

I think if I left Kevin and Lora alone for more than a week there would be no saving this house from destruction.

Okay, I wasn't much better.

I left my bras all over my bedroom. My breasts hurt like crazy if I tried to wear one. A very, very cruel man must have invented under wires and I know I could probably find something to wear maternity wise but it was just better to let them go free.

I needed to get the house more baby friendly anyway. I was now entering my thirty-fourth week of pregnancy and I didn't even have a crib yet. I hated the thought of asking Lora for the money to buy a crib. I couldn't ask her for that. She did enough for me... and to be honest, I worried about the epic fight we might get into later because I couldn't believe she took Kevin to the bar without telling me about it first.

I decided not to focus on my lack of funds. Everything needed to be spotless in the house. I could worry about a crib and baby stuff later but first I needed to make room for it. I couldn't do that if the house remained dirty.

I started by placing all the dishes in the dishwasher. That was easy. I didn't even bother pre-rinsing them. I would wash them again if they needed to. I hated touching half chewed food. It was disgusting.

Lora kept most of the cleaning supplies on top of the cabinet above the sink. There was about a foot of space between the shelf and the top of the fridge where we kept paper towels, paper plates, and vitamins up. It was hard for me to reach any of it because I was a good three inches shorter than her. She could just hop on her foot stool and get what she needed, but I had to use a chair.

I stared at the old, rickety looking thing. I had to stand on it a few times to reach what I needed already. I just hadn't needed to in a few weeks and now my stomach was bigger.

I shook my head. I had to climb on the stupid chair.

This was ridiculous.

I wasn't *just* going to scrub the stove clean,

I wanted to tackle the entire house. I looked underneath the sink, and of course nothing but the dish washer liquid was underneath with a bucket, so I decided then that I would move everything under there. After that I needed to rearrange some of the food in the cabinets because I could never find anything I needed, and I needed to wash everyone's laundry because it seemed like it piled up into a never ending heap in the bathroom. But first, I bagged up the trash and took that outside.

When the hell did I become a Susie homemaker?

Oh. Right. Pregnancy does that to a girl.

I was thinking too hard. I needed to stop that and the only solution I could think of was to turn the radio on full blast on classic rock and to get to cleaning.

~*~

Aidan

Mom thought Briana might be pregnant.

She took a pregnancy test.

I guess I understood why she took off like a bat out of hell.

I drew in a deep breath. I had to keep myself together. If I let myself be distracted I might drive into a tree or something.

As it was, it took me too damn long to get up the balls to risk driving to Lora's house. She would have to tell me where Briana was, especially if I could catch her off guard by letting her know I knew Bri took the pregnancy test. I would refuse to leave until I had the answer. Hell, maybe I'd just end up being lucky, and Briana would actually be there. Maybe I wouldn't have to drive all the way up to Kentucky to try to find her. Crazy enough, I would do that if it's what I needed to do. I did the math and figured that she would be about eight months pregnant. *Eight months.* My stomach rolled at the thought. Had she convinced herself she couldn't trust me or something?

Shit. I was nervous. It took me everything not to just drive to Lora's as soon as Mom told me what she thought happened. I almost called Cynthia to ask her to come with me. Briana hurt Cyn just as bad as me when she left without another word. Cyn worried about her on a daily basis even though neither one of us talked about it much. I almost think that's why Cyn threw herself into planning her wedding so hard. She did that whenever she was upset or had something she didn't want to think about. She threw herself into projects, whether it was something small she had to do for class or something as life changing as getting married.

I didn't think I'd face this situation again so soon. I hadn't thought about the baby Cynthia didn't keep in a long time. It hurt too damn much. Oh, god, I thought, what if Briana didn't keep it and that is why she wanted to hide from me?

No, I couldn't think that way.

I sucked in a deep breath. I needed to calm down since I was going over there. It wouldn't do either one of us any good if I got myself all worked up before I even got to the house. It would be worse if Briana wasn't actually there.

For the moment, I decided to think of something else. Like Blue Moon. Mom was right. I loved that horse. I took the sale ad for him off the internet as soon as Mom left my apartment. She got pretty pissed off at me for that and hadn't responded to any of my requests for Dad to put her on the phone. I just counted my blessings because Mom didn't actually know how many inquiries had been sent to me asking about possibly meeting so people could buy him.

I deleted every single one. Hell, Briana would want to kill me if she found out I'd wanted to get rid of him. She loved my horse. I knew she did, even though she got hurt riding him a few months ago.

Shit. Thinking about something else obviously was not going to work. I couldn't.

Instead, I focused on driving. It wasn't too long to get to Lora's place and I was thankful that I at least remembered where it was. I tried to think of what I could think or say to make Briana know things were okay. I wanted to, but couldn't, be angry at her for taking off. She got scared. She had so much on her plate already that I couldn't blame her. I didn't exactly give her a reason to believe that I would stick around if something happened. I wondered why she wouldn't try to talk to me, and why she would cut me off like she did, but that wasn't something I could let myself question or else

I'd drive myself crazy.

Eight months pregnant.

I drew in a deep breath and pushed my hair out of my face. I just hoped she was there, and that Lora wasn't the one who opened the door. Maybe Kevin answered it I could get him to listen to me. I liked that kid. He had a good head on his shoulders despite some of the crap decisions he made in the past that caused Briana to move in the first place.

There was only one car in the driveway when I got there. It looked kind of like the one Briana told me she had before she moved here. Did that mean her aunt got it back for her?

I slowly pulled into the driveway, turned my car off, and took in a deep breath.

I don't know how long I sat in my car wondering why the hell I decided to come to Lora's house. I didn't know what I would do if Bri wasn't here. The woman threatened to call the cops on me the last time I saw her. I didn't want to worry about that kind of shit… but I didn't see Lora's car.

What the hell? When did I ever care about doing something that would get me into trouble? If I stayed scared of everything I would have never kissed Briana in the first place. I wanted to know where she was, how she was doing… if she was pregnant with my child. I climbed out of my car and slowly walked up to the front porch, my stomach turning itself in knots.

I knocked on the screen door. I could hear music so I knew someone was home, but I just couldn't see inside very well because of the small hallway that lead off in the small foyer. The music had to be coming from the kitchen.

"Hello? Is anyone home?" I asked, knocking again.

No answer. I looked around, feeling like a dumbass because any normal person would have called someone living there by now to let them know they were coming. A lady with two small children walked past us and looked at me funny. I gritted my teeth for a moment and then decided to hell with it and tried the screen door.

Not locked.

Was whoever was here expecting someone? My heart raced a little, hoping that maybe it was Briana that was home. The car in the driveway could have totally just been Lora's car, as in maybe she had gotten a new one, but I had to believe that Briana was actually here and that I wouldn't walk in and scare the shit out of Lora. She really would have a reason for calling the police on me then.

I followed the sound of the music after I closed both doors.

Sure enough, Briana was there. Her red hair had grown, loose around her shoulders. I just stared for a minute, completely forgetting what I wanted to say to her, what I thought I wanted to say to her, the moment I saw her. All I could do was stare at her stomach, forgetting that at first all I could do when Mom told me she thought Bri might be pregnant was to be angry. Bri's baby was my baby, too, and I had a right to know. But then I started to think about it and I realized she really had every right to be scared about this. I didn't know what made her leave like she did, but I absolutely intended to find out.

I simply stared.

"You're a sight for sore eyes, baby."

"I—what—ah!"

Briana turned around quickly in the chair she'd been standing on. She lost her footing and started to fall back. I acted quickly, not thinking about anything else other than the fact that she was about to bust her skull on the tile and that it would entirely be my fault.

I caught her underneath her arms, the chair flying in the other direction.

"Shit," Briana said, her hand flying to her chest.

"Shit is right," I said. "Are you okay?"

"Um," Bri stammered.

She tested her feet and managed to stand. I kept my arms around her, which slid down to her bulging stomach. I didn't know it was so possible for my heart to race the way it did. Shit. She really was eight months pregnant.

"Um, Aidan," she finally said, clearing her throat. "You can let me go now. I'm fine."

"Oh, yeah," I said, removing my hands from her body like she burned me. I didn't know what to think, or what to say to her, and I felt incredibly stupid. I couldn't believe it didn't occur to me that she could still be living with Lora or that she could be pregnant sooner. "Why were you standing on that chair?"

"I, um, had to move the cleaning supplies." She pointed to the top of the fridge. "Short girl problems. I can't ever reach anything."

"You're not short," I said, chuckling.

"Well," she brushed her hair out of her face. "The fridge is too tall then." She stared at me for a second. "I'm sorry, how did you get in here? Or even find me?"

"How could you stay with your aunt and think I wouldn't eventually find you?"

She wouldn't look me in the eyes. Instead, she looked down, and placed her hand over her stomach to rub it.

"Did, um, Lee and Nikki tell you?"

"You're telling me my cousin knew before me and he didn't tell me anything?"

"Nikki found out and she's become friends with him, I don't know. They showed up here Friday night wanting to talk to me."

"I'm gonna fucking kill him."

"Don't do that, I pretty much swore anyone who knew about it to secrecy."

I needed to breathe. I took a step away from her to pick up the chair. The thing was rickety as hell. Why did she think it would be okay to stand on it? I sucked in a deep breath and released it slowly, telling myself that she must have been scared when she found out she was pregnant. She might have been doing what she thought was right for the baby even though that made absolutely no sense to me what so ever. I wanted her to be my girlfriend. It'd been a while, but I even thought I'd asked her if she wanted that. I told her I loved her. I wanted to ask her so many questions but I didn't know where or how to start.

"What happened, Bri? I think I deserve some answers." I said, instead, settling on that.

"I don't know," she said.

"What do you mean? Did you think I wouldn't want you to tell me you're pregnant with my baby?"

"Yeah, actually," Briana said, suddenly all sass and fire. She stood up straighter and put her hand on her hip, tilting her head to the side. "I don't think you're ready for the responsibility of a baby... especially since you made Cynthia get an abortion a little over a year ago."

I felt like the wind got knocked out of me. That's what this was all about? That's why Bri stood there, completely stiff, like she wanted to run from me. She thought I wouldn't want the baby.

"Bri..." I started, moving forward. She took a step back but I wouldn't let her go. I grabbed her hand. "*No*, baby, how could you ever think I made her get an abortion?"

"Well, she told me she got one. I naturally assumed it was... Oh, god, Aidan, I'm sorry."

"Bri, Cyn wasn't ready for a kid. That was *her* choice. I tried to talk her out of it but she wouldn't listen. Why would you ever think I would want you to get rid of it?"

Bri cleared her throat. "Him. It's a boy."

"We're gonna have a little boy?"

She looked up at me, nodded. She let me

pull her a little closer.

Next thing I knew, I pulled her in and we started kissing. It had been too long since I kissed this woman. I knew I missed her but I didn't realize how *much*. Her lips were soft and welcoming, warm and intoxicating, as I pushed my tongue into her mouth. She kissed me back just as passionately, pushing her body into my chest as well as she could with her pregnant belly. I didn't stop her when she took my shirt off, or started to lead me toward the living room. My knees hit the back of a couch and she tore her top off, her beautiful breasts spilling out. She didn't have a bra on, and they'd gotten bigger due to the pregnancy. Briana was a beautiful woman but it was like the pregnancy made her glow, as corny as that shit sounded.

This wasn't exactly making love. We hadn't seen each other in months. I kind of think her hormones were driving her crazy. That shit happened when women got pregnant, right? It drove them crazy? It was like she was hungry for me, and only me, and the only thing I could think was how badly I wanted her to climb on top of me.

I got my jeans off as fast as I could, my dick springing free. Briana stared at it for a second before she wiggled out of her pants, and I helped. I pulled her close, kissed her stomach, just thankful that she was there and not in Kentucky where it might be harder to find her.

"Wait," I said, standing. I leaned down and kissed her. "This won't hurt—"

Briana shook her head. "Don't worry. I—

don't talk or I might talk myself out of this."

"Bend over," I said instead, thinking that might be more comfortable for her.

She climbed onto the couch and grabbed a pillow. It took a little maneuvering, but I managed to get into a comfortable position. We barely spoke. We just wanted to feel. I stopped just at her entrance, wanting to be sure she was ready. The last thing I wanted to do was hurt her and my heart raced.

"What are you waiting for?" she asked, pushing against me, sounding almost frustrated.

I laughed. "Eager, huh?"

"I can just get dressed…"

I grabbed her hips, gently keeping her in her place. "No, don't…" I groaned as I entered her. "You're not going anywhere."

Briana

I was in my bed.
With Aidan.
I couldn't tell if the dizzy feeling swimming around in my head was a result of being pregnant or from being with him, again, finally.

Doggie style on the couch wasn't the most comfortable way to make love, so we moved it to the bedroom. Halfway between an orgasm and realizing what time it was, I decided it would be safer to have sex in my bedroom rather than risk my brother or aunt walking in on us.

I breathed calm, and deep. His arms were warm, and big, and wrapped around my chest. We had to talk to each other. We had to say something. I just didn't know what I wanted to say to him.

"You're shaking," Aidan said, pulling my comforter up to my shoulders.

"I'm not cold."

His hand couldn't stop wandering to my belly. Our baby fluttered and kicked inside as if he recognized that mommy and daddy were actually together. When did I become a cliché, I wondered? A part of me wanted to tell Aidan to get out, but another part of me just wanted him to stay so much more. I couldn't even give myself a good reason to make him leave.

"You're scared, aren't you?"

I turned as well as I could. It wasn't that it was hard to move around yet. I didn't even feel gross and I'd heard some pregnant women at the doctor's office complaining about how much they wanted the pregnancy to be done. But I guess that would be in the later weeks?

"I'm not sure if this is real," I said, finally.

Aidan laughed softly and pushed my hair out of my face. "Not real?"

"You should be screaming at me, not making love to me."

There. I said it. One of the reasons I avoided him for so long was that I worried about how angry he would be at me for not telling him I got pregnant. I hated yelling. But he was here, and he wasn't yelling, and it confused the hell out of me.

"Why would I *ever* scream at you?"

"I wasn't going to tell you…"

Aidan took in a deep breath. "I'm not happy you kept it from me. We have a lot to talk about, but I want to enjoy being with you right now."

"We're idiots. We should talk about this. I have a serious flight issue and you have a history of being in an open relationship and we both have serious trouble with communication."

"So? Everyone can be an idiot sometimes but that shouldn't mean that we can't try to work things out and be together."

For the first time since I found out I was pregnant, I suddenly felt a sense of clarity I hadn't before.

"I got scared. *Really* scared."

"I wish you would have just talked to me." Aidan propped himself up on his hand and looked down at me.

"It was a lot to take in. I fell off Blue Moon, your mom and girlfriend bombarded me with a pregnancy test, and I found out Cyn had an abortion all within the span of an hour and a half."

"Shit," Aidan said. "Please don't ever call Cyn my girlfriend again."

"What?"

"I thought you knew."

I shook my head, feeling like an idiot all at once. "No no no, I know she's engaged to Lee. I knew you were broken up."

"Why did you change your number and let everyone think you moved?"

"Panic, Aidan. I've been panicking this whole time. I dropped out of college and I've been dealing with a lot of crap. I…I'm worried Lora is drinking too much and Kevin is dating and I'm pregnant. I've felt like I've been panicking for months and I just can't stop."

Aidan released a deep sigh and bent down, kissing me.

"We'll figure things out. You panicked. It's okay. People panic all the time for less."

He was right. Something told me I shouldn't trust him so easily again but I told that part of me to shut up. Aidan was a good guy. A *really* good guy. My son would need his father. Aidan deserved to know his son.

That didn't mean I couldn't stop doubting myself, though.

"I don't want to rely on you," I said. "I refuse to do that. I don't want to be a house girlfriend. I decided to take a break from college for a semester because I knew I'd need the time for the baby. I keep putting too much ahead of other things to earn my degree though."

"Baby, you can do whatever you want to. I'm not going to stop you from having an education or doing what you want."

I stared at him, wondering why I ever thought there was anything to worry about.

"Things are *really* over with Cynthia?"

"She's engaged to my cousin. There's a definite coffin in the relationship."

I released a huge sigh of relief. "Good."

"That doesn't mean I don't still care about her. I'll always care about her, and she's about to become a part of my family."

"Is it weird that she's with Lee?"

"Hellishly," Aidan said, laughing. "God, I wish you would have told me sooner."

I closed my eyes, moaning lightly as his hand ran down my bare stomach just above my pelvis. I thought I got horny sometimes before but now it was like I couldn't get enough of Aidan. I wanted to not let my head get foggy with hormones but I hadn't seen Aidan in months.

His hands jerked away at the sound of a loud bang on the door.

"Oh shit," I said, "Kevin might be home."

I scrabbled to get out of the bed.

"Oh, shit," Aidan said. "My jeans are still out there."

I flushed, wondering how I would explain *that* one. Instead I threw a shirt at him, and some boxers, from my closet.

"These are mine."

I must have turned the color of a tomato. Actually, I looked into my mirror, and I was more like a fire truck engine red, if that were even possible.

"I guess a few things of yours got mixed in with my stuff when Nikki packed them for me."

He looked at me, amused. "I couldn't be mad at you even if I tried."

I smiled at him and pulled on some pajamas. Walking through the living room, I quickly grabbed our things and shoved them in the most inconspicuous place I could find... inside of the big ass coffee table that I always stubbed my toe on. It worked. I may have bent a few magazines in the process but it wasn't like Lora ever read them.

The knocking started again, and this time it actually made me jump. That wasn't the knock Kevin would use. Besides, he had a key. I saw him put his keys into his backpack on the way out of the house. What was I thinking?

I opened the door.

Outside, John and aunt stood. Lora looked irritated about something, rifling through her purse.

"This is so annoying. How did I manage to lose my keys?" she looked up. "Bri! I'm so glad you're home."

"You don't have your keys because I took them away from you," I said, stepping away, making room for them both to come inside. "I thought that you would be coming back home like three Fridays ago."

"I decided to stay at John's. What are you all of a sudden? The fun police?"

Keep calm, I told myself. I didn't understand why she was suddenly acting so hostile with me but it didn't make sense. I pushed my hair back, very aware that my shirt was out of place and that my pants were still not pulled all the way up.

"Why are there clothes all over the place?"

"That would be my fault," Aidan said,

leaning against the wall.

    I turned bright red.

    "Aidan! I—"

    "What the hell are you doing here?" Lora asked immediately.

    "Long time, no see, Lora." Aidan stared my aunt down, still so betrayed by the fact that we hadn't let him know I never moved out of Kentucky. "I thought your niece moved to another state."

Chapter Ten

Briana

Lora and Aidan stared at each other. Utterly terrifying, it was like a wild cat and a wolf eyeing each other down, trying to decide who would strike first.

My aunt made absolutely no sense to me. She wanted me to tell Aidan he would be a father. She'd tried to encourage me to tell him about my son, but she hadn't dropped the adoption issue either because she didn't think I would be able to do everything I wanted to in life if I had a baby.

"I thought I told you that you aren't allowed on my property again."

"You're really going to call the cops on me when you lied about Briana being in Kentucky?"

"I was for a little bit," I said, swallowing thickly. I really hoped Lora was in a mood to argue and nothing else. I don't know if I could handle it if she actually decided to call the police on Aidan.

"Excuse me for trying to protect my niece," Lora said, scoffing loudly. She closed her eyes and stumbled a little, throwing her purse onto the couch. "I think you better leave. I'm not in the mood for company right now."

"*Lora!*" I gasped. "What is wrong with you?"

"It's called partying too hard," Lora said, "and living a little. I don't understand how people have kids."

I didn't know this woman right now. I sniffed, and realized there was a faint hint of bar surrounding her.

"Briana, come here," Aidan said, reaching for me.

"Um, we need to let her sleep it off," I said, following him back into my bedroom.

I turned around for a brief moment. Lora groaned and laid down, her hand holding her forehead. She definitely had a hangover.

"Yeah," Aidan said.

"I'm really sorry, Aidan."

"It's okay, Bri. If I had any idea you were going through this I never would have let you leave."

"I didn't give you a choice did I?"

We stared at each other for a few seconds.

More than ever, I regretted my decision not to let him know about the pregnancy. It made me feel like crappy person. Aidan wasn't the type of man who told many people that he loved them, but the way he held my hand and seemed like he was moments from pulling me into a hug? I could feel how much he still loved me; how much he'd missed me.

"Um, maybe you should go. I need to go pick up Kevin since he has school in the morning."

What the hell was wrong with me?

Aidan took a step back like I'd slapped him, but I couldn't let myself feel sorry for him. I really did need to go pick up Kevin. I worried that Lora would decide she really wanted to fight with Aidan too. Or, worse, she would mention the fact that she wanted me to give my son up for adoption. I couldn't deal with that kind of stress right now. I already felt—stupid? ...foolish? ...silly?—since I slept with him again right off the bat.

"Okay," he said. "Yeah. I guess I'll see you around."

He leaned down to kiss me but I turned my head and he kissed my cheek.

"Yeah," I said. "I'll see you around."

"We need to talk."

I looked back up at him. "I know," I said. "We will." I quickly grabbed a piece of paper from my dresser. "Here," I said, writing my number down. "I'm sorry I changed it on you."

"Oh." Aidan grabbed the paper like I might decide to take it back from him. "Yeah, thanks.

Why did you change your number?"

I sighed. "I really don't know."

"I wish you would have told me as soon as you found out."

"I needed space," I said.

"Well, we definitely need to figure things out. Have you had enough space?"

I hated myself.

"I'm not sure if I have. But really, I need to go pick my brother up. We'll talk later, okay?"

Aidan

So many things hit me at once on my way back to my apartment.

Briana was pregnant. We had a son on the way. Lora claimed her title as a certifiable bitch. Cyn and Mom kept the fact that Briana took a pregnancy test from me this whole time when we could have possibly avoided months of me wondering where the hell Briana disappeared. I had to wonder just how many people had been lying to me about that very thing the entire time.

Nikki, obviously, but she was Briana's best friend, and we'd never spent a lot of time together. I tried not to bother her much about where Briana went, and I wasn't going to harass her now for answers to all the questions that kept running through my mind.

Briana needed space, and she might still need space, so I had to try to give it to her. That didn't mean it would be easy. I fucking missed her, and I hadn't realized how much I actually missed her until I saw her in her kitchen trying to reach something by using a wobbly kitchen chair to get what she needed.

There were things I didn't know yet, like what she was going to do now with our son on the way. What about supporting herself? Something inside of me didn't want her to rely on Lora, not after what I'd seen at their house. I wanted to be there for her in any way I could. Bri seemed determined to keep me at an arm's length, though, and I didn't know what I could do to fix that.

I hadn't realized I'd driven to Cynthia's apartment until I was near her street near Shiloh University. If anyone could give me answers, it was Cyn. She'd listen to me. She knew, more than anyone, how I felt about becoming a father one day because she took that opportunity away from me once. She broke my damn heart when she had the abortion and that's one of the main reasons why our relationship didn't survive.

I had a choice, I could've turned around, but instead I turned onto her street and parked in front of her apartment. Her mother still needed to borrow her car, so she still didn't have one. I hoped she wasn't out with Lee or something. That might make my getting answers a little difficult. I knew he still didn't really trust me around Cyn most of the time but I thought it was bullshit. I didn't want her.

Screw it, I decided. I got out of my car and

walked to Cyn's door, and knocked.

Kari, Cyn's new mousy roommate, answered the door. I didn't know her well because she rarely spoke or left the apartment. I knew Cyn repeatedly tried to get her to look for a new roommate but the girl didn't seem like she cared that Cyn would be moving out at the end of the semester into my old apartment.

She had no initiative and barely got to class on time, and it was a wonder how she would even survive the rest of the semester, let alone survive in their little hole underneath a beautiful town house by herself. Cyn's words, not mine.

I really didn't know the girl that well. I might have subconsciously avoided getting to know her in order to avoid another situation like what I ran into with Briana. Cyn hadn't let up on trying to get me to date other women.

"Um, hi?"

Definitely mousy, I'd give Kari that. She had a type of earthy-crunchy hippy vibe to her. If I didn't know what dread locks were, I might have suggested she go brush her hair.

"Is Cyn around?"

"Are you one of her boyfriends?"

What the hell did the girl mean by that?

I decided to leave it alone. Cynthia was far too faithful to mess around on Lee. She talked about nothing but her wedding to my cousin and had even tried talking us into trying on suits last week.

"God could you be any more nosey? Cyn

said, pushing the girl out of the way to open the door farther. "Aidan? Aren't you a sight for sore eyes?"

We both ignored Kari's griping when someone moaned loudly above us when I walked inside. Christ, did those people ever stop having sex? The frantic, almost desperate look in Cyn's eyes when she glared up at the ceiling, a broom in her hand, told me everything. She'd been trying to study and couldn't because of loud neighbors. I'd bet her roommate was driving her up a wall, the way Kari glared at her and took a seat on the futon.

"I have *no* idea how you can listen to that," Cyn said, turning to her roommate.

"Ear plugs," Kari said. "Did you really have to push me? I almost fell down."

"Eh...sorry." Cyn turned to me. "Get me out of here. *Please.*"

"Having trouble studying?" I asked, chuckling at her.

"You don't even know. Why'd you show up anyway?"

I wasn't sure if I wanted her to know Briana was really pregnant, not when I wasn't sure how she would really take it because we'd almost had a child together. I really just needed to get over myself with that. Cynthia could handle the news just as well as anyone else.

"I just needed an old friend," I said. "Want to go to the Roadhouse?"

Cynthia beamed. "Absolutely!"

She paused for a second, rolled her eyes,

and looked at Kari when the girl huffed.

"Do you want to go too? I'll get you a beer."

"I'm *nineteen*," Kari said. "That's illegal."

Cynthia gave me a look.

I had to laugh at her on the way out to the car. She would never change. If someone did something Cyn didn't like, they automatically became someone she didn't care to have anything to do with ever again. Kari would be lucky if she got to keep the apartment after Cyn and Lee were ready to move in together. I wouldn't put it past her to let one of her other biology friends move in under Kari's nose.

Cyn couldn't help but be a bitch. I looked at the way her father was and it made sense. It was one of the reasons we weren't still together. At the same time I knew I would never have to worry about her being able to take care of herself.

"So what made you decide to come pick me up out of the blue? You haven't done that since we broke up."

"I guess I needed a break," I said. "We were friends before we really started dating. Maybe I miss that."

I turned in the direction of the Roadhouse, our unspoken place to always get a few drinks together whenever we had the time to spend together. I almost hoped Samantha and Bobby were there too. I didn't know if Briana wanted other people to know about her being pregnant but she'd have to get over it. Cyn, Bobby, and Sam were some of the most important people in my life, and I didn't know if I could deal with the knowledge that I'd be a father soon without freaking out about it.

"Something's wrong," Cynthia said. "What's up?"

"Briana is pregnant."

Cynthia sat up so fast she banged her head on the top of the car.

"OW!" she yelped. "What?!"

"She's pregnant."

"You found her?"

"It didn't take me a lot to figure out that she was still staying with Lora when I went there and saw her."

"You SAW her!?"

"She's eight months pregnant. Are you okay?"

Cynthia rubbed the top of her hair then smoothed it back. "I'll be fine," she said. "I'm more worried about the fact that Bri is *pregnant* and we didn't know about it."

"Mom said she took a pregnancy test before she left."

"Oh. Yeah. She did."

"Why didn't you tell me?"

"I don't know," Cynthia said. "Was I supposed to? I didn't think things would drag out this long. I figured Briana did freak out, but she would come back eventually…"

"Cynthia," I said, knowing her better.

"Okay," Cyn burst out. "I was afraid that I might have talked her into getting an abortion."

"Why the hell would you say that?"

"You know how I've felt about kids in the past," Cyn said.

I decided not to touch that one. For the first time in a while we were actually talking to each other and I didn't want to ruin that. I missed Cynthia. Missed her friendship, and her unique view on the world.

"You'll work things out with her," Cyn said, taking my hand in hers. She kissed my knuckles and then put my hand down quicker than I could give a proper reaction. "Do you finally have her number again?"

"Yeah," I said. "I'm fucking terrified. What if she decides I can't be a part of my kid's life?"

"If she decides that she doesn't want you to be a part of the baby's life then just sic Aberlie on her."

I burst out laughing.

"Oh god, Mom and a pregnant Briana. That worries me."

"You'll get to see your child," Cynthia said. "Ain't nothing gonna come between Aberlie and her future grandbaby. You know how much pressure she put on me to finally settle down with you when she thought we were still happy together."

I grinned at the thought. Mom had been relentless. As her only child, all the pressure fell on me to have a lot of children she could spoil.

"Why don't you give Lee a call?" I asked. "Tell him to come have a few drinks with us."

"I'm not sure where he is tonight," Cyn said. "I tried calling him but he hasn't been answering his phone for the past day or so."

"That's weird," I said. "He's usually good about answering his phone. Has Mom said anything?"

"I haven't talked to her because I've been trying to study for an important test for the past few days," Cynthia said.

"Right, sorry," I said, shaking my head. I couldn't always keep up with Cynthia anymore but I wasn't going to tell her that. "Well, listen, we haven't really spent a lot of time together since we broke up, so why don't we just spend the night catching up? Maybe I'll let you talk me into making an appointment to get fitted for a tux."

"Really?" Cynthia asked, excitement in her voice. "That would be awesome."

Maybe that wasn't such a good idea either.

Fuck it, I made the suggestion, so I'd let Cynthia dress me in a tutu if that would make her feel better. Something was bothering her tonight, and it didn't take a lot for me to realize it had something to do with the way she talked about Lee.

Especially when we walked into the Roadhouse and saw him with an arm around Nikki at the bar, a pissed off Sam glaring at them like she wanted to bash a rum bottle against my cousin's head.

"What the *hell* is this?" Cyn asked.

Briana

Robin's parents had a fancy suburban house in one of the nicer parts of town and it genuinely surprised me when I parked at the end of the cul de sac. Usually her mother dropped her off or picked her up.

Even more surprising; Kevin sat on their steps. Usually it took a while to get him and Robin to say goodbye to each other.

I rolled my window down.

"What's going on?" I asked.

"Fucking Freeman," Kevin said. "He's in there right now. Begging her to forgive him."

My eyes widened. "The kid who picked on her?"

Kevin opened the back door and threw his backpack in. He slammed the door so hard that it rattled me in the front seat.

"Hey!" I said. "Easy on my car! I don't care how angry you are."

Kevin didn't seem to care because he slammed the front passenger door too.

"Do I need to go in there and kick that kid's ass?"

"No," Kevin said. "I'm done with Robin. She wants to be with an abusive dick? She can be with the asshole. I have come too far since moving from Kentucky to let some asshole ruin my chances of finishing school on time by getting expelled for bashing his head into a fucking wall."

"Language," I said, even though I didn't really mean it. I agreed with my brother, all right. I couldn't believe this was going on, but then again,

Kevin never really talked to me about it. I realized I'd been so caught up in my drama with Lora, Aidan, and the baby, that I hadn't stopped to ask my brother how things in his life were going. "Do you want to tell me what happened exactly?"

"Robin and Freeman dated for a while. They slept together and then he started spreading nasty rumors about her online."

I didn't like the sound of that, not one bit.

"The only reason she's going back to him is because her father wants her to," Kevin said, angrily. "He apparently doesn't like that I have a pregnant twenty one year old sister who is perfectly capable of making her own decisions. Oh, yeah, and Mrs. Freeman is in there right now."

"I don't think we need you to worry about getting expelled from school," I said, seriously considering getting out of my car. "I might have to go kick someone's ass myself."

"Can you just drive, Bri? I made some money over the weekend helping one of Robin's neighbors with his computer. I want to forget about it. I'll get you some beef jerky."

Beef jerky?

That was all it seemed like I wanted anymore, and the baby kicked, like he agreed with his uncle Kevin. I decided to leave the issue of

"Aidan knows about the baby."

"What?"

"Yeah. He knows. He came over and…yeah. He came over."

"You did him, didn't you?"

"Kevin," I scolded.

"What? I'm glad he finally figured out what's going on. Now I don't have to call him douche nozzle anymore."

"Okay can we not go on an Aidan bashing spree? It's not his fault that I got pregnant and didn't tell him. Just because you had a shitty time with Robin doesn't mean that you need to bash the father of my baby."

I'd snapped at him, and even though I didn't mean to, Kevin needed to hear that. He turned a little red and sank down into his seat, looking well and truly put in his place.

"I didn't mean that," I said. "I didn't mean to bring what happened with Robin into this."

"Let's just go get your beef jerky."

I decided I was a horrible sister.

"Watch a movie with me tonight?"

"Sure."

Well, maybe not so horrible.

~*~

Aidan

"What is this?" Cyn pointed frantically between a cozy Nikki and Lee. "Are you seriously kidding me right now? What, are the two of you on a date?"

Samantha made eye contact with me, the both of us deciding to take a step back while Lee and Cyn hashed things out. I'd only step in if things started to get out of hand; a very real possibility if

Cyn got a hold of either one of them.

Cyn didn't care if it was a man or woman, if she decided their ass needed kicked, it got kicked.

"Cyn, baby, this isn't what you think it looks like…"

"Like *hell* it's not what I think it looks like!" Cyn burst out. Several other customers in the bar started to stare. "I can't believe this! I really can't believe this, Lee! I thought we were really happy!"

"Well you know what? I'm pretty pissed off at you because you knew there might be a possibility that Briana was pregnant and you didn't tell Aidan!"

"Hey now," I said, "don't bring me into this."

Nikki gawked at me.

"You're not freaking out?" She turned to Lee. "Why is he not freaking out about finding out he's gonna be a daddy?"

"Because he already knows, you moron," Cyn said. She grabbed Lee's drink out of his hand, what looked like straight whiskey, and knocked it back. "I can't believe this. I seriously can't." She slammed the glass down onto the bar and started to fuss with her left hand, trying to get her engagement ring off. "That's it. I can't believe—"

"Hey, why don't we all try to calm down?" I tried.

"There's no way I'm going to calm the hell down!" Cynthia shrieked.

She lunged toward Nikki but I acted fast, locking my arms around her waist.

"You need to chill the hell out," Nikki said,

taking a step back.

"Aidan! I swear if—"

"I don't care what kind of threats you make, we aren't sticking around long enough to see if you can get yourself thrown in jail, Sinner." I picked her up and threw her over my shoulder.

She hit my back as hard as she could, bursting into tears. "Put me down!"

"Uh… Thanks." Lee said, merely staring at me.

I reeled back my fist and slammed it into his face.

"Don't fucking thank me, you piece of shit," I said. "You had something really fucking good and you're wasting it?"

I shook my head, not giving a shit that everyone stared at us or that Samantha finally had to ask us both to leave. I couldn't believe he did that.

"Are you going to put me down yet?" Cynthia asked when we got to the car.

"I don't know. Are you going to tear in there like a banshee to claw off Nikki's face?"

"I don't know," Cyn said, sniffing.

"Well then I'm not letting you down."

"I won't go after the stupid bitch," Cyn said, huffing.

I put her down.

"I'm sorry, sweetheart."

"Your cousin is a jerk."

"I could've told you that," I said, hugging her.

More sniffing. "Can I spend the night with you?"

"Sure. I'll sleep on my couch."

"Aidan…you don't have to do that."

"Well we're not sharing a bed," I said.

Cyn pulled away. "All right. I just don't want to be alone tonight."

"Well, you don't have to be."

"I feel like I should get revenge on Lee."

"Well, get your revenge, but it ain't gonna be with me. I have to think about Briana and the baby."

Cyn roughly wiped tears from her face and stomped to the passenger side of the car.

"All right," she said. "You're right."

The both of us got into the Nova and for a moment I thought she would be okay, other than crying. I wished I would have done more than punch Lee in the face. I wiped blood from his nose on my jeans and started the car.

Chapter Eleven

Briana

I didn't want to wake up. The last thing I wanted to do was drag my butt out of bed after a small morning nap. I had things to do but getting out of bed seemed like so much effort. I had to stop by the high school and drop off a few things for Lora because of her drinking problem. I had to do more grocery shopping, too, and I heavily considered driving out to see Aidan because we had things we needed to work things out.

>Aidan: Think you're going to come out today?
>Me: I'm not sure. I have to run a few errands first.
>Aidan: I think it would be awesome if you came out... did you hear what happened with Nikki and Lee?
>Me: I knew already. I knew they would get caught, and told

> her not to do it. Is Cynthia okay?
> Aidan: I'm worried about her. She'd love to see you.
> Me: She still staying with you?
> Aidan: No, she finally went home.
> Me: I can't believe she stayed with you so long.
> Aidan: What else was I going to do, kick her out?
> Me: No... But she does have her own apartment.

I tried not to be annoyed when Aidan told me that Cynthia would be staying with him a few days. I *did* become annoyed when it became an extended stay a week and a half later. They weren't together anymore, and they were just friends. I didn't even know if I had a right to be jealous because of the fact that I wouldn't tell Aidan what I wanted one way or the other. He'd asked. I never responded. That wasn't a conversation I wanted to have through text messages. I'd recently decided to stop letting little, petty things get in the way of me being with Aidan. I couldn't believe I'd taken so long to let him sway me into coming to visit him. We'd wasted enough time.

> Me: I want to see you.
> Aidan: I know a horse who misses you too.
> Me: I would love to see Blue! Um... your Mom isn't going to freak out on me is she?
> Aidan: I haven't told her yet.
> Me: Lovely.
> Aidan: Please just come out here? There's something I want to show you anyway.

Not knowing what else to say, I didn't respond, and instead chose to climb out of bed so I could get my day started. I didn't want to give Aidan a definite "yes" yet because I wasn't certain how long everything else would take, but I didn't want to give him a flat out no either.

Was fear a large deciding factor in that? Yeah, it was.

~*~

Aidan

"This is impressive," Mom said, walking around the house.

I'd thrown myself into getting a few last minute things done and now all that needed to be done was to paint. I hadn't quite decided to tackle that yet. I still couldn't figure out what to buy as far as paint colors went because they were all named such weird fucking things. I couldn't get the fact that there were actually paints named Embricardo and Shangri La out of my head.

"You just need to paint and you'll be set."

Her boots thudded softly on the newly set wooden floors.

"So you want to tell me why Cynthia has been staying with you at your place?"

"Nothing is happening, Mom."

"All I know is that Lee came back, pissed off to high hell with a broken nose, and said she left with you. Please don't tell me you're going to get back with her."

"Mom, I found Briana."

If it were possible, my mother's eyes might have popped out of their sockets.

"Is that so?"

"Yeah. She's definitely pregnant."

"So help me god, Aidan, if you do something that is going to keep me from ever meeting my grand baby I will—"

"Mom," I barked, "nothing is going to happen with Cynthia. We're friends."

"You say that now," Mom said, "but I've heard you tell me that before, over and over again. You let her drag you back down every time something isn't going right in her life and I'm sick of it—"

"Lee cheated on her."

That stopped Mom in her tracks. Her face turned red and her eyes grew wide, like she couldn't believe that her golden boy Lee would ever be able to do something like that to a woman he claimed to love. Angrily she crushed the few paint samples in her hand.

"Say no more," Mom said, releasing the paint samples from her grip but still held them. She spent the next few minutes trying to smooth them out. "Back to Briana, you should tell her to come over for dinner."

"Now listen, she's been scared out of her mind. If she does come over I don't want you to do anything to upset her."

"Why would I do a thing like that?" Mom huffed. "I knew she was pregnant the minute dog food made her sick. I'm not one to judge another woman for running and neither is anyone else in our family. It took your father until I was seven months pregnant to come around and it wasn't until after you were born that I fully forgave him."

I knew that story. Mom liked to bring it up in the middle of dinner sometimes to shame my father for something else he did, if she wasn't threatening to withhold sex and make him sleep on the couch.

"Well, we'll see if she shows up. She said she might. I think a few things are going on that she's not telling me."

"Like what?"

"I think something is up with Lora. The two of them almost bit each other's heads off when Lora got home the day I found her."

"Her aunt always seemed irresponsible." Mom fiddled with the paint samples in her hands. "Anyway, if Bri shows up, I'll be ecstatic, but I think I can round up a few friends from church to help get the rest of the house finished."

"Yeah? I can try to pay whoever offers."

Mom shook her head. "I don't think we'll need to do that. Everyone always jumps to help. All I have to do is tell them we're busy because we need to get you a nursery finished fast."

"Mom..."

"Don't you 'Mom' me. The two of you are having a baby together. That girl loves you."

"She hasn't even said it to me yet."

"That's the whole reason you've been in such a funk for the past few months, son. You need to try to work things out with her."

Mom smiled at me then turned and walked out of the house.

I wish things were that simple, but they weren't. I pulled my phone out of my pocket and looked at the time. Almost noon, and Briana hadn't sent me a response back yet. I was about to go to her but I decided this was one of those instances where I shouldn't push her to do anything. Bri could be a stubborn girl, and if pushed hard enough, she would eventually decide she didn't want to have anything to do with me. That was the last thing I wanted.

"Fuck it," I said to myself. Instead of sending Bri a text, I called Bobby.

~*~

Briana

Sometimes I thought about what might have happened had I stuck things out in Kentucky. What would have happened had I decided to move to another city, like Richmond or Lexington? Would I have really had a big problem managing Kevin on my own then? I certainly wouldn't be unsure about my education, and I wouldn't be pregnant.

I slowly eased my hand across my belly, instantly angry at myself for thinking about that. My son—Aidan's son—was a blessing, but I couldn't help but think over what Lora suggested once in a while. What would happen if I gave him up for adoption or just let Aidan have him?

I shook my head at myself. Overthinking became tiresome after a while. Lora needed her crap—how does a *teacher* forget to bring her gradebook with her?—and I needed to get on the road to go see Aidan.

I'd decided to go see him. The thought terrified me, but I knew we wouldn't be able to avoid each other forever.

"You've *got* to be kidding me," I gasped.

Lora's room was empty because this was her

planning period. Planning future classes and grading her student's work must have been the last thing on her mind. Instead of doing anything that a teacher might normally do—I had no idea because I never really stuck around long enough to talk to my teachers when I was in school—she instead had her heels kicked off, her feet propped up on her desk, and a bottle of whiskey in her hand.

"Oh, shit," Lora said, sitting up fast. She quickly put the cap back on her bottle and then shoved into the top drawer as fast as she could, motioning at the same time for me to quickly close the door.

"Did you forget I had to bring your grade book by?"

"Are you kidding me? I never do grading during planning time."

"Don't you think that's a little irresponsible?" I asked, pulling the book out of my tote. "I also got your Kindle and a few of the other things you asked me for."

"Awesome, thank you."

"I think I might try to work things out with Aidan."

I blurted it out before I could even stop myself. Lora looked up at me, shook her head, and opened her drawer back up.

"Oh come on," I said, running my hands through my hair in frustration. "Is it really a bad thing that I want to keep my baby and work things out with his father?"

"I wanted so many things for you, Briana. *So* many things." She opened up her bottle and took a big swig, "including becoming a mom one day, but I figured that wouldn't happen until later. Not *now*."

"Yeah, well, things happen in life that we have no control over." I crossed my arms and shook my head at her. "You have a drinking problem."

"I don't, I just have a problem with my brother being dead so he can't talk sense into you about this whole having a baby thing."

"That's *it*," I said. I didn't care if I was pregnant or if it might get my aunt fired, I reached forward and took the bottle away from her.

"Hey!"

"You are *embarrassing* yourself. What will you do if someone comes in here and sees you drinking like this? My God, how could I ever trust you to take care of my brother when you aren't taking care of yourself?"

Don't burst into tears. Get angry, I told myself. Get good and angry. Lora deserved it.

"If you don't straighten up then you're never going to see me or Kevin again," I said, the words burning my mouth like hot acid.

Lora was one of our only relatives left alive other than my grandfather and I didn't *really* want to lose contact with her but I would if it was better for my brother and my son.

"And you definitely won't see your great nephew. I do not like your boyfriend. You need to break things off with him."

"The hell I'm going to break things off with John," Lora said.

"Ah," I said, taking a step back toward the entrance of her classroom. I couldn't stand arguing with her. I needed to leave. "I thought you didn't want anyone to know what's going on."

"You need to get the hell out of my house."

I poured the bottle into the trash and then slammed that in there too. "*Gladly.*"

Oh, hell, what had I just done?

Five minutes.

I let myself have five minutes to freak out about Lora basically kicking me and my brother out of the house. She hadn't seemed very sober, so there was a chance she wasn't completely serious, but I wasn't going to let the one little chance that she *was* serious possibly mean that my brother and I would end up living in my car.

Who was I kidding? I wouldn't be living in a car. I would find some kind of entry-level job before I let myself become homeless. I hated how over imaginative I could get sometimes. I hadn't had one single urge to write for the past few months since I'd found out about the baby, but that didn't mean my creative mind would ever stop turning. I actually thought about writing for the first time, but that came with the worst timing ever.

"Hey! I was wondering if you were ever gonna get back in touch."

Aidan's voice instantly made me forget about my new five minute rule. Something about it soothed me. I hadn't noticed before. Missing someone does that; it makes it easier to notice things that might not have popped out before. The way his slight southern drawl made him drag out his words, made him seem calmer even though he must have been going crazy waiting for me to make a decision about whether I wanted to see him or not.

"Have I ever told you I'm in love with you?"

My throat went tight, the complete opposite of what I thought would happen when I eventually broke down and told him the truth, like crying? Definitely thought there would be a lot of crying. I waited, breath baited, hoping he would answer me and finally have a little mercy.

"You have no idea how long I've been hoping you'd say that."

"Well, I do." I said. "I love you."

"Are you okay?"

I shook my head even though he couldn't see me.

"I just got into a really bad fight with Lora. She's drinking, at a *high school*." I cleared my voice. I sounded too weak. "She threatened to kick me out."

"Oh hell, Briana."

"I can't stay with her anymore, Aidan. I just can't. I don't want to. I don't want our baby to grow up in a broken home with a great aunt who drinks too much. I don't want Lora to be a role model to Kevin anymore. I'm tired of her making me feel like shit because I'm pregnant and want to keep our baby. Did you know she has actually been trying to get me to give him up for adoption?"

"For one, sweetie, calm down."

I huffed. "I don't want to calm down. Why should I calm down? Just because I'm pregnant doesn't mean I have to keep myself calm and lay down all the time and—"

"Baby, you're hyperventilating."

I sucked in quick gasps of air so fast I almost sounded like I was doing crappy labor breathing than hyperventilating.

"Oh," I said, forcing myself to stop and take in a deep breath.

"Second, I love you too."

"We'll make things work."

"We will. I think we need to have a talk."

"I hate that, 'have a talk'. That's what couples say to each other before they're about to break up or something equally awful."

"I didn't know we're a couple, Bri."

"W-well."

Damn.

"You're right. We need to talk."

Aidan burst into laughter.

"You're cute when you're all flustered."

"I am not flustered. I want to kick Lora's ass but I can't. I hate this."

"No, we can't have you kicking her ass."

Things only seemed worse than they were right now. It would get better, and I had to make myself believe that it would. What did I think would happen when I had the baby? Spend the first year leeching off my aunt and expect her to support me, my baby, and my brother until it was time for me to grow up and start acting like an adult again? No. It was a good thing that Aidan was back in my life.

"We'll talk when you're here," Aidan said.

"Okay." I started my car. "Wait, maybe I should check Kevin out of school. I don't know how serious Lora was about kicking us out."

"Do what you need to. I wouldn't mind seeing

him. You know how Mom is. She'll make enough food for a small army. Mom actually wanted to have you over for lunch anyway."

"That sounds great," I said. "See you soon."

Aidan

Why the hell were my hands sweating?

I hadn't even been off the phone with Briana for ten minutes, and already I'd turned into a nervous wreck. I fed the horses quickly, having no patience for Blue Moon when he decided to be a smart aleck and grab my hair.

Fuck it. If he wasn't going to stop that shit, I'd just cut it.

I had far more important things to worry about.

"Mom, Briana is coming out here," I said, bursting into the kitchen. The rabbit scurried underneath a table past my feet. Mom calmly looked up at me, in the middle of cutting up some carrots.

"Well it's about time she decided to show back up."

"Don't," I said. "I'm just glad we're talking again. She told me she loves me."

Mom smiled. "Well, maybe things will work out. I told you they would."

"I really hope so," I said. "I guess things have gotten really bad with Lora. They got into a fight and Bri was pretty upset."

"Y'all can take as much time as you need talking."

"Can you make sure there's enough for Kevin too? She's checking him out of school early. I guess Lora wants them out of her house."

"What a selfish bitch," Aberlie said, shaking her head. "I had a feeling she was the sort and I've never really met the woman."

"Listen, I don't want to judge the situation. I am just relieved she's coming out here and that we'll finally get to talk."

"No problem. I'll even entertain her brother if you decide to go have a walk."

"Lee isn't going to be here tonight, is he?"

Mom immediately scowled.

"Your father actually had a few words with him about how he treated Cynthia."

I had to take a step back. Dad never acted like he gave a damn about what Lee did, and he certainly never acted like he cared about Cynthia, so talk about a shock.

"What do you mean, he had a few words?"

"He told him to get the hell out and go back to his parents."

Lee still lived with Mom and Dad.

"Is that why so much shit is left undone today?"

Mom wiped her forehead with the back of her arm. "Yeah. Lee went. Your father told him he best get out of here for a week or so before either of you decide to muck the stalls with his ass for the way he treated Cyn."

"Why are you telling me this now? Why not, oh say, when it happened?"

"I'm so mad at your cousin I haven't bothered

to think about where he's been," Mom said, chopping some more vegetables aggressively. "I'm not Cyn's biggest fan but she doesn't deserve to be treated that way, not after all she's been through."

"Invite her to dinner tonight," I said. "I'd do it myself but I have to go get a shower... and just how the hell does Dad think we're going to manage without Lee around?"

"I guess I'm hiring a few college students to help us get the work done. I've needed a few more stable hands anyway."

I thought about calling Lee to see how he was doing but decided against it when the urge to punch the stupid fucker came back full force. I wanted to worry about Cynthia, and I wanted my stupid ass cousin to realize how much he messed up, but I had more important things on my mind.

Briana and the baby had to be my top priority from now on.

Chapter Twelve

Briana

I'd forgotten how beautiful the ranch was.

I hadn't been here since fall, with the leaves changing and falling out of trees. The grass dulled in color and it called for time to get out heavier coats. Now it was definitely spring, with new leaves and a blooming magnolia tree next to the mailbox. The grayish clouds above spoke of possible rain. A sharp kick from my son reminded me of what a fool I'd been. I should have decided to get in contact with Aidan sooner. I kept arguing with myself the whole drive over while Kevin slept in the seat next to me, trying to remind myself that I wasn't a terrible person for keeping my pregnancy from Aidan for almost eight months.

My hands were clammy, and the overwhelming urge to turn around and work things out with Lora overcame me. This was the first time I would see Aidan's family in months. The last time I saw Aberlie she shooed me into the bathroom to take a pregnancy test right after I fell off her son's horse.

No. I refused to chicken out.

I'd realized something pretty important on my drive down here.

Lora didn't matter.

She could tell me to give the baby up for adoption, threaten to take custody of my brother, do whatever the hell she wanted to. She wasn't really in our lives before Mom and Dad died. I loved but nothing she said would ever fly in court because all I would have to do is bring up her drinking problem. It would be low, and she would never talk to me again, but after the way she had been acting, I no longer wanted her to be around us, and especially not my son. I needed to stop relying on everyone, get my damn degree, and be the best mom and sister I could possibly be.

Something about Aidan—no, something about *being* with Aidan, the thought of him, the way he made me feel and made me think, it made me *want* to be that better woman. I felt so stupid for dropping out of school for a semester because I got scared by getting pregnant. Maybe it was the pregnancy hormones, or I'd grown up within the past eight months, but now I'd started to think more clearly. Talking to Aidan was my main priority tonight, and something told me he wouldn't completely shut me out like I originally feared. It was a silly fear. I needed to stop giving a damn about what everyone thought.

I parked next to the Nova, my clammy hands full on sweating now that I'd actually parked, and rubbing them on my jeans to get rid of the excess moisture didn't help.

"Hey," I said, "we're here, Kev."

I shook his shoulder in an attempt to wake him up. I hadn't realized he'd fall asleep so fast after I checked him out of class. He refused to really talk to me after we got in the car and I couldn't figure out why he insisted on being in such a good mood. I figured Robin had a part in how he was acting but I didn't feel like I should pry.

He groaned, opening his eyes. I grinned at him, wondering how he could fall asleep whenever he wanted. His hair needed to be cut; he wiped it out of his face at least three times before he stretched and groaned.

"I'm sorry, sis. You shouldn't have let me fall asleep."

"It's okay," I said. "If you're tired, you're tired. I'm not going to take away from your beauty sleep."

Fully awake now, he glared at me.

Giggling, I opened the door and shoved my keys into my pocket. Maternity jeans were weird and I felt like I was wearing a cheap knock off jegging but at least they fit well enough. I missed my normal jeans and didn't even want to think about how they might not fit for a long while.

"I'm a guy. I don't do beauty sleep."

"All right," I teased, "whatever you say."

"My God, your belly has gotten huge."

I quickly looked up at the sound of Cyn's voice.

I hadn't expected her to be here, but realized that was silly, because she worked for Aberlie. She was a part of their family even though they might not exactly admit it.

"Well, hey to you too."

She shook her head, dropped some hay to the ground and pushed her hair out of her face. "Geez, I'm sorry. That was so rude. It's just been a while."

I shut my car door. "Yeah, I know it has," I said, smoothing my hand over my belly. "Almost eight months."

"Yeah," Cyn said. "Well, everyone is in the house. I was just bringing some hay up here for the chicken coop. Aberlie has a few pullets she's ready to put outside in the garage. Let them know I'll be in there in a few minutes?"

"Yeah," I said.

"Hey, Sinner."

"Don't you start, little boy," she said to my brother in a teasing tone.

Rolling my eyes, I laughed at them both and headed toward the house.

"How'd you know her nickname?"

"Aidan calls her that all the time. I don't think he realizes how much."

I didn't even have to knock on the door. Aberlie flung it open, a smudge of flour smudged on her cheek. She had a huge smile on her face and her eyes brightened when she looked down at my stomach.

"Oh Bri," she said, reaching forward and pulling me into a huge hug, "I don't know why you thought you had to run away the way you did."

I swallowed, getting choked up for some reason. Maybe it was the way she said it, like she was upset that I hadn't thought to really let her in. Aberlie always just sort of oozed this maternal energy and I could feel it then as she wrapped her arms around me.

"I got scared."

"We all get a little scared sometimes," she said.

"I'm hungry," Kevin interrupted.

I rolled my eyes and stepped back from Aberlie. Kevin's surly attitude wasn't going to go anywhere any time soon.

"Can I help with anything?" I asked, knowing how hard Aberlie worked to make dinner for the family at the end of the day.

"No baby, you're fine. Aidan is back in his old room if you want to go hunt him down."

"Okay," I said. "Sounds good. Oh, Cyn said she's putting some hay in the chicken coup and then coming inside."

"She's still fussing over those chickens?" Aberlie shook her head.

"Care if I watch some TV?" Kevin asked.

I chose to head in the direction of Aidan's room, wondering where Lee was because he usually had his butt parked in front of the television whenever I came here if he wasn't working outside. It was getting late though, so I imagined that the hay being put in the chicken coup was the last thing that needed to be done for the night.

I started to knock on the open door frame where I found him leafing through an old, worn leather bound book, but changed my mind and decided to just watch him. His boots were off, kicked near the night stand and his hair wasn't in its usual pony tail. He had a little mud on his right knee and his hair looked a little rough, like Blue had decided he wanted to take a nip out of it again. Giggling gave myself away even though I still wanted to keep watching.

He looked up and grinned at me.

"Hey," he said, closing his book. "I was worried you might not actually make it."

Shrugging, I walked into his bedroom. "I looked at the book, trying to read what it said on the spine. "What were you reading?"

"Ah, it's nothing. Just some Peruvian love poetry."

I grinned at him, picking it up. "Love poetry, huh?"

"Yeah," he said.

I grinned at him. "Cool."

"So Lora kicked you out?"

"Cutting right to it, aren't you?" I asked, sighing. The last thing I really wanted to think about was Lora but it was something that *had* to be thought about. "She's just drinking too much. I can't take it anymore."

Oddly enough I didn't feel like crying about it anymore. It was almost like crying over spilt milk; not worth it. It wasn't worth my time. When had caring about Lora's well-being become a low priority? I sucked in a deep breath and let Aidan wrap his arms around me at that realization.

"I'm done with her. It's like she's changed recently and I don't want my fifteen year old brother around that kind of influence. She took him to a bar, Aidan. A *bar*. I don't want him thinking that's okay."

He kissed the top of my head and squeezed me. The baby kicked and I buried my head into the corner of his neck, breathing him in. He smelled like a mixture of his favorite shampoo and hay.

"Listen, that kid has a stronger head on his shoulders than I think you give him credit for. From the sounds of it he's as frustrated with Lora as you are. I'd be more worried about our son growing up in that kind of environment."

I looked up at him. "No way in *hell* am I keeping the baby around her if she's going to keep acting this way. I'm not sure what I'm going to do but I'll be damned if she thinks that will happen. I don't even know when I started to rely on her so much. I hardly knew her before I moved to Tennessee. I mean, we talked on the phone, and she liked to joke that I was just like her, but if she's going to keep partying and drinking, and possibly lose her job? I get that she lost her brother, but I lost my *Dad*, but I'm not going around being an asshole like she is. I'm grateful for what she did when I moved down here but sometimes I wish I would have thought it out better before I moved because I didn't realize how unreliable she could be."

"Well, don't go throwing stones at her yet. She's got a problem, baby. She needs help. Have you thought about suggesting rehab?"

I pulled away from him and shook my head. "I'm done. I'm washing my hands of Lora. I just can't do it anymore. I'm not sure where I'm going to live, but I'm definitely not going to live there anymore."

"Well...I don't know if you'll—"

We both turned around at the sound of a knock on the bedroom doorframe. Aidan's Dad stood there, a glass of whiskey in his hand, scrubbing his face while he warily looked in the direction of the living room.

"Dinner's done," he barked out.

"All right, Dad," Aidan said.

"You are pregnant," he said to me.

I smiled and looked down, rubbing my hand over my stomach. "Yeah."

"What is it?"

"A boy."

"Quit being a dumbass and marry her, son."

My cheeks flushed and his father walked away. Where did *that* come from? I never figured his father to be a man who spoke more than a few words or to have nothing else to do but to criticize everyone else around him. The way he said "marry her" kind of sounded that way, but it was more like he was actually trying to give advice than anything else. Aidan looked bright red too and I had to laugh because I hardly ever saw him get embarrassed.

"Someone take that whiskey away from Dad!" he barked down the hall. "Jesus, Bri, I'm sorry."

I burst into giggles. "It's okay. Funny that he's loosened up a little."

"Yeah, but we were just talking about your aunt drinking too much and in comes—"

"I highly doubt your Dad will do something to hurt himself though."

He rubbed his face. "Yeah," he said. "He just likes a glass every once in a while. He's still pissed at me for going through a bottle of bourbon around Thanksgiving."

"I'm sorry I left," I said. "I just... I need to get that out there."

"All right," he said. "Dad had the right idea. Maybe we should get married."

I immediately shook my head. "No," I said. "I don't want to get married. I know that's ridiculous because I'm pregnant, but I don't want to get married just because I'm about to have a baby."

"Be my girlfriend then."

I grinned at him, reached for his hand and pulled him to me. "That I can live with." I stood on my toes and kissed him quickly.

"We're not done talking yet."

"No, we're not. We have a lot of things to discuss. I'm starving," I said. "Let's worry about that later."

He chuckled at me. "All right. Mom is making barbeque chicken."

My mouth immediately watered. "Really? I've been craving that lately."

"Have you?"

"Are you kidding me? It's been forever since I've eaten chicken, Kevin and Lora are so damn picky."

He burst out laughing. "What other cravings are you getting?" he asked, putting me in front of him as we walked out of the bedroom. He put his hand on my stomach to feel it. "Does he kick a lot?"

"On the cravings: chocolate and beef jerky. I *can't* get enough of it. He kicks all the time, no one has really felt it yet. It depends on where he's been kicking." I grabbed his hand and moved it over. "His head likes to sit there a lot."

Aidan's breath tickled my neck as he felt the baby bump. "I'm tempted to say we should skip dinner so we can talk."

"Nope," I said, shaking my head. "I'm far too hungry."

"Alright," he said, laughing.

~*~

Aidan

I couldn't stop staring at Bri when I sat across from her at the kitchen table.

They say women glow when they're pregnant, and she was definitely glowed. Mom pretty much couldn't stop talking about how cute she was since she was pregnant and how she couldn't wait to meet the baby. Bri had surprised us, and was now passing around her last ultrasound.

"Oh my gosh," Cyn said, her hand flying to her mouth. "He's going to be so precious."

I studied my ex-girlfriend for a brief moment, wondering how she was holding up. I'd told her earlier that Bri would be coming over and at first she seemed like she didn't want to stay for dinner like she usually did.

I wasn't even sure why she came in for work that day because she'd told me it was hard to be around the family after the way Lee cheated on her. Sometimes I wondered about that girl, and what she'd do after she was done with school. I hadn't really talked to her lately. She'd be fine, I decided, so I went back to staring at my girlfriend.

I wanted her to be a whole lot more than that.

Dad had the wheels turning in my head. Bri told me she didn't want to get married just because she was pregnant but I had to wonder if I shouldn't just go ahead and ask her anyway. It didn't matter that we hadn't been together very long; she was the one. I loved her.

"Well," Dad finally said, speaking up. "It's all fine and good that we're going to be grandparents, but I need to talk to you about those horses, Aberlie."

Mom's eyes narrowed at Dad immediately.

"Oh hell," I said, rolling my eyes. "Not this shit again, Dad."

"What about my horses?" Mom said.

"We need to sell a few stallions." Dad said.

"Like *hell* I'm selling any of my horses just because you say so."

"We have too damn many."

"Will you give it up?" Cynthia said, rolling her eyes. "There's no way in hell you're going to get any of those horses sold right now. We need them since the trail riding is about to start back up."

"I don't know why you're worried about it," Dad said. "You're graduating here in a few months then you'll to be running off to a fancy vet school."

Cyn looked down and pushed her hair out of her face. "I'm not so sure that will happen. I might stay a while and work."

I looked at her in surprise. "What do you mean, you're not sure if you want to be a vet?"

"Oh good lord, don't tell me you're quitting that dream just 'cause my nephew is a dumbass."

Kevin and Bri looked at each other

uncomfortably. I couldn't blame them. They weren't ever the type of people to just throw their problems with other family members out in the open.

"Um, where is Lee, anyway?" Bri asked.

"I kicked his sorry ass out," Dad said. "I ain't going to have anyone living under my roof—"

Mom cleared her throat.

"—our roof," Dad corrected, "when a bunch of unnecessary drama is going to be kicked up."

"Oh," Bri said.

"Um, can we not talk about him?" Cyn said.

"Of course sweetie," Mom said, glancing around the table.

I hadn't said anything yet, but I'd decided to show Briana the house. It was a little dark out but we had the electricity back on since most of it was finished except for painting the walls. I wanted her to move in with me, even if she didn't want to get married. Maybe I would wait on that. I didn't have a ring and I knew she wanted to finish school even though she wasn't going right now. I'd be talking to her about that too. There was no reason Bri shouldn't finish her education. I'd looked into what sort of stuff Kevin would have to do if he transferred to my old high school too out of curiosity a while ago. It might take a bit for him to adjust, but they would transfer all his school credits and he would be able to move on in the next grade level if Bri decided to move so close to the end of the school year.

"Hey, Bri?" I said. "Want to go for a walk?"

Her plate almost empty, Bri grabbed a paper towel from the middle of the table and wiped her face even though nothing was actually there.

"Sure," she said. "Can we go see Blue?" Her face brightened up at this, like she couldn't wait to see him.

"Yeah," I said, "if we can find him."

She stood up so fast I had to laugh at her because her belly got in the way and she bumped into her plate. Mom grinned at me the entire time because I helped Bri by grabbing her water so it wouldn't spill on the table, then pulled out her chair further so she could get up easier. Bri wasn't that big yet but she always had that clumsy side and it seemed like it was worse now that she'd gained weight from pregnancy.

"Oh geez," she said, turning red. "I'm turning into a whale. I'm sorry, Mrs. McCoy."

"Now," Mom said, putting her fork down, "I think with you having my grandbaby, it should automatically be established that you can call me Abs or Mom."

I loved it when Bri turned red. You could see a few light freckles easier when she blushed and it made her hair pop out. Her hand never seemed to leave her stomach now.

"Okay, I'm sorry, Aberlie."

"Now, don't go apologizing either," Mom said, laughing at her. "Answer one thing for me before you two go off outside?"

Bri and I looked at each other, Mom's question perplexing me just a little bit. I didn't want to be embarrassed anything, but knowing my family, anything was possible. Dad already couldn't keep his mouth shut and told me to marry her already. So far they'd been pretty decent but I'd also had a talk to my parents before she got here and asked them to behave themselves because I wasn't sure what Bri would do if she thought anyone was angry with her.

"Go ahead," Bri said, smiling wide at Mom.

"Am I gonna have a little grandson or granddaughter?"

Briana's smile widened and she looked at me. "Should I tell everyone, Aidan?"

She had an infectious smile. "I'm not sure..."

"Now don't you go playing that coy shit with me," Mom said, obviously about to burst. She pointed at Kevin. "I'm sure he knows."

"I'm still not sure..."

"It's a boy," Kevin blurted. "Geez, Bri, don't drag it out on them."

"You ruined my fun," Bri pouted, playfully cuffing her brother on the back of his head.

"Oh my," Mom said. She jumped up so fast that she spilled her drink, squealing. She made her way around the kitchen table, reaching for Bri, who stumbled when Mom pulled her into a hug. "A grandson! I might pee, I'm so excited!"

Everyone in the dining room burst into laughter, including myself.

Chapter Thirteen

Briana

"On second thought, maybe it wasn't a good idea to walk out here."

I stopped. My back hurt like hell and we weren't even where Aidan wanted to go yet. He wouldn't tell me either and it frustrated me.

"You all right?"

"I just need a minute," I said. "I forgot what a walk it is to the other barn."

"Oh damn," Aidan said, smacking his forehead. "I totally forgot. I should've driven us out here."

I raised an eyebrow at him. "Really? You're thinking about that *now*?" I grinned

"Sorry," he said, easing an arm around my

waist. I leaned against him, feeling a little out of breath. I'd been sitting around too much. That had to be part of my problem too. "Do we need to turn back around?"

"No," I said, leaning against him. "We don't need to. I just need a minute."

"All right," he said.

"Where are you taking me anyway? I mean, besides going to see Blue?"

"You know, he might be out here," Aidan said, looking over my head. "I'm not sure. I let him go in the pasture earlier."

We'd been walking along a fence line since there was a road that Aidan could have *easily* driven on. Don't get mad at him, I told myself. He wasn't thinking. He was probably still adjusting to the fact that I'd gotten pregnant and sometimes men just don't *think* the way women do. Though, to be fair, I wasn't really thinking either. I'd learned that a long time ago because that's what Mom always said whenever it came to Dad doing something that pissed her off. I just didn't realize how *right* she was until I started seeing Aidan.

"Ugh. My feet hurt too."

"Want me to carry you, big baby?"

"You try carrying this kid to full term," I griped.

Aidan laughed at me. We walked up to the fence where I promptly leaned my back against in order to catch my breath. Aidan didn't let me go. I'd noticed he'd been doing little things like that since I got to the ranch, like he couldn't keep his hands off me. I can't say that it bothered me a bit.

"Aidan, I can't apologize enough for taking off like I did."

I needed to say it. I *wouldn't* ever be able to apologize to him enough. He'd missed so many things in our son's development so far and I didn't like myself for it.

"It's okay Bri," Aidan said. "A lot happened to you at once. You were stressed out. I probably wasn't helping anything by flipping back and forth so much between you and Cyn."

I shook my head. "You know, it wasn't even really that, Aidan. I was okay with it. I understood. Honestly I'm surprised she's not trying to get back with you now that things with Lee have gone south."

"She wouldn't do that," I said, shaking my head. "She knows we'd be ending our friendship quickly if she tried something again." He pressed his nose against my neck, paused, and then kissed the spot that used to make me moan like a wildcat in bed. It still made me moan a little, the sound getting caught in the back of my throat. I almost forgot for a second that my back hurt and that I was pregnant. "I'm in love with you, and not just because you're pregnant. I fell in love with you long before that."

I turned to face him so I could stare into his eyes. "I should have told you that I love you a long time ago."

"You need to quit apologizing."

I laughed. "I feel like I need to."

He pushed some of my hair out of my face. "You don't need to, baby. You have nothing to apologize for."

"Well, I guess not."

"You feeling better?"

I sucked in a deep breath and nodded. "Yeah, I think I'll be able to make it now."

"It's not that much farther."

"Where are you taking me?"

"It's a surprise."

I groaned. "I don't like surprises, you know."

He grinned and I finally understood a few stories pregnant women told about having sudden violent urges to hit the father of the child. Mom threw a fresh apple pie at Dad when she was pregnant with Kevin. I remember it well because I was almost seven or eight when it happened. Dad licked the stupid pie off the door and it made mom angrier.

"You better watch pissing me off," I griped.

"I'm pissing you off, huh?"

"Yep," I said to him. "Better watch it. The women in my family tend to throw food when we're pregnant."

His laugh was deep, and it echoed while we walked off in the direction of wherever the hell it was that he was taking me.

We walked for at least twenty more minutes, talking about everything that came to mind, from how the horses were doing, to when Cyn's graduation date was, to what it was like when he went to see his grandmother for the holidays. I felt like crap because I upset him so bad that he stole an expensive bottle of his Dad's bourbon and felt like general shit the whole time those first few months because I wasn't there.

"You know, Cyn actually talked me into going on a date around Valentine's Day."

My face turned red, and not because I was embarrassed.

"Oh," I said, my voice turning a bit stiff. "How was that?"

Aidan burst into laughter. "It was awful, Briana. I couldn't even remember her name and I talked about you the whole time."

My entire body relaxed. "Really?"

"Yeah, baby. The girl never wants to talk to me again."

I laughed. "It's her loss then."

Aidan stopped. "Wait a second," he said, stopping me on the road.

I looked around. It seemed like they'd recently laid down fresh gravel, and the house was near the barn where they keep the Kentucky Mountain horses. I hugged myself, confused, because I thought he wanted to take me to see the horses first but we'd walked far past the barn. The fence to the pasture where I knew he kept Blue Moon continued to run along the road and it looked like some mulch had just been down a little further on the road on the side. A large oak tree that I hadn't seen before sat in the middle of the pasture. I hadn't ever been up this far on their property, not because I wasn't allowed to be up here, but because there hadn't ever been any need for it.

"Why haven't I seen this part of the ranch before?"

"Mom is particular about this area."

"Oh?"

"Yeah. Would you think about moving in with me?"

I can't say I hadn't been expecting that question but it still took me for surprise. "Well..."

"Wait. Dad was right about something. We don't have to get married, but I feel like I should be there to help you with the baby if you need it. You will, Briana. Kids are a handful, especially a baby. You know some about what that's like because of your brother but it's different when they're your own. My uncle's wife just had a kid and she's called Mom several times stressed out so bad she wants to pull her hair out even though she loves the kid. That's not just why I want you to move in with me, though. I'm in love with you, and I feel like we've wasted enough time being stupid about the entire thing. I never wanted the open relationship... Cyn did."

Bri knew this. I needed to remind her anyway.

"Aidan—" I tried again.

"No, please, just listen, just hear me out. That is all in my past, but I know it was something you were worried about when we started getting closer. Please, Briana, don't let us lose a chance to be together because we're both afraid we're going to screw it up."

I wasn't sure if I wanted to cry or smile, so I simply reached for his face with both of my hands and kissed him. He kissed me back, soft, slow, passionate. This kiss meant something more than it did when we first saw each other again.

"I would love to live with you," I said. "I don't think your tiny apartment could handle a teenager and newborn, though."

Aidan grinned like a Cheshire Cat. I stared at him, fascinated, when he grabbed my hand and started walking me down the road again. I had no trouble keeping up but my loose tennis shoes made it hard to walk on some of the bigger pieces of gravel and I stumbled, walking after him like a clumsy, pregnant oaf.

"Slow down a little," I said. "I'm getting fat and can't keep up with you."

"You are not getting fat," he said, "you're beautiful."

I rolled my eyes, and then gasped.

I'd heard once that there was another house on the ranch, but I'd never thought to ask to really see it before. No wonder Aberlie was particular about this part of the property. The house was a picturesque ranch house with blue shutters and a wraparound porch. It was nicer than the one his parents lived in now, so I stared at Aidan in confusion, wondering why he was showing this to me. Were his parents going to move into it or something?

"This is ours, if you want it to be."

"What?"

"Yeah," he said. "I've been working on it a few months. I got tired of being cramped up in the apartment and I thought Lee and Cyn were going to move into the place so I started working on it. It was hell not knowing where you were, Briana, so I needed a project."

I gaped at the house. There were even the beginnings of a flower bed started, Aberlie's touch, I imagined.

"Oh wow," I said. "Of course I'll move in with you."

"If you're worried about the high school or anything it's a decent one," Aidan said. "Mom and I have already looked into it for you. Kevin would be fine there."

"You know," I said, wrapping my arm around his waist when we started walking toward the house, "I'm not worried about Kevin. I think he'll be fine. I'd like to stop moving him around so much but I think he needs a break from the school that he's in now."

"You're probably not wrong," Aidan said. "He broke up with his girlfriend, right?"

I nodded. "Yeah. I feel awful for him."

"Well, he'll meet plenty of other girls," Aidan said. "I want you to go back to college."

I laughed. "Yeah… good luck to myself on that one. I don't want to throw all of the responsibility on you while I'm in school. You're busy enough."

Aidan laughed. "If you think for one minute that Mom isn't going to be willing to watch our kid then you're mistaken. I've already talked to her about it. She said she wants you to go back to school. I know that's something you're worried about…Cyn was worried about it too."

There wasn't a way we could continue having this conversation without talking about Cyn and the abortion, and we both knew it. My son kicked at that moment, almost like he was irritated I wasn't paying much attention to him.

"Oh," I said, my hand flying to my stomach. "He just kicked hard."

Aidan's hand immediately went under my hand. The baby kicked again.

"Whoa," he said, "I felt that one. I thought he liked to keep his head around the other way."

"He turns a lot when he's not sleeping," I said. "I'm just so used to it by now that I usually don't notice it until he kicks me."

The baby kicked again, as if he were trying to prove a point. I laughed.

"I think he approves of mommy and daddy moving in together."

I grinned. "I guess he does…"

"I don't want to show you the inside yet."

"That's not fair."

"It's not painted."

"I don't care." Maybe I want to help pick out the paint."

Aidan grinned. "You do, huh? Mom is going to get some help painting from some volunteers from her church."

"Well, I know I'm not supposed to help

paint, but I definitely want a little say."

Aidan kissed me this time.

"Of course you can help."

I wrapped my arms around him, just needing him to hold me for a second. Things were going far too well for me to be completely comfortable but I decided to just go with it. I'd missed Aidan, and I didn't want to keep making the mistakes I'd made before. I didn't even want to think about what it would have been like if I moved back to Kentucky. Kevin and I would have done well, I was sure, but that was the furthest I was willing to really go in the thought process. I didn't want to go through the thoughts of my son not knowing his father. That would be wrong, and it wouldn't be rational on my part.

"Well," I said, my hand running down Aidan's arm to his hand, where our fingers interlocked. "Since you won't show me the inside of the house just yet, want to show me the barn?"

I nibbled his ear.

Aidan

Sometimes I had dreams about fucking Briana in the barn.

I wanted to make love to her in the house, but it wasn't ready for her to see yet. That meant she might find out what Mom and I were planning for the nursery and I wasn't ready to drop that surprise on her yet. The easiest way for me to make her forget was to pin her up against a stall door, like I was doing to her now. She became easily distracted with my fingers up inside of her while I bit her neck.

"Aidan," she gasped. "What if someone comes looking for us?"

"They won't," I said, unzipping my jeans.

"I can't let you—"

I stopped for a minute, swearing. We had to be careful because of the baby and I knew it.

Then I looked at some of the hay that I threw down earlier for the horses.

"Fuck it," I said, kicking off my jeans. I led her inside the stall. "The damn horses never come in here anyway. You know they're so much less maintenance than the thoroughbreds?"

Bri's laugh had always been infectious, but it turned sexy as hell when she moaned after I laid her down and went back to teasing her with my hands.

"Lift up," I said, tugging on her pants, no longer in the mood to just mess around.

She did, and she got out of her shirt and bra too. Careful not to put too much weight on her, I reached for those perky breasts, which had gotten larger, and squeezed.

"Gentle!" she griped through a moan.

"Uh…"

I jumped off Bri as soon as I heard Kevin's voice, swearing under my breath, struggling to get my pants back up. She still struggled to get her clothes back out when I popped my head out of the stall to see Kevin standing there with a bright red face.

"Uh," I said, "what's up?"

"Damn it," Kevin said.

"Watch your mouth!" Bri gasped out.

"I mean—shit—sorry!"

"Stop swearing!" she hissed again.

I didn't know whether to laugh or be embarrassed myself so I tried my damnedest to keep a straight face. Clearing my throat, I straightened out my shirt then stepped out of the stall.

"Is something wrong?"

"Yeah," Kevin said. "John called. Lora got into a wreck."

Chapter Fourteen

Briana

My hands shook; it felt impossible to get my fight with Lora out of my head. All I could think about was how she told me to get out of her house and how I gladly agreed that I needed to leave. We'd done nothing but fight since I got pregnant and it only got worse when her drinking became out of hand. I knew she had a problem and I still did nothing to try to help her. I felt like the worst niece on the face of the planet and I didn't even care that my back hurt when I burst back into Aberlie's house to find my purse.

"Briana, slow down," Aidan tried. I wouldn't listen to him. All I could think about was how I had to get to the hospital, and fast, to make sure Lora was okay. I had so much I needed to do. I needed to call

Grandpa. I needed to kick John's ass for letting her drink so much. I needed to stop being a child and tell Lora I would stay with her and make sure she got better. "Come on baby, do you really think you can drive right now?"

My legs didn't feel steady but I shook my head.

"No, Aidan. She's my aunt. I need to get out there as fast as possible."

"I have to agree with him, sis. You need to calm down!"

"Maybe you should sit down," Lee tried.

What was I thinking when I agreed to move in with Aidan? Everyone would always be in my face during my pregnancy, always concerned and convinced of my fragility. That's how it felt anyway while I continued my search for my purse.

"Now hold on," Aberlie said, grabbing my wrist.

"What?" I said, turning to look at her. "I need to get to the hospital. My aunt was just in a wreck."

"Sweetheart, you're hyperventilating," she said.

I stared at her.

"In a panic attack? Please just sit down before you send yourself into an early labor."

When had I started sobbing?

I also had a headache. Damn.

Aberlie wouldn't hear anything of it. She made me sit, and I didn't fight her on it. I felt woozy all of a sudden but all I could think about was how I wanted to go check on my aunt.

"Here." Cyn kneeled in front of me and shoved

a cup into my hands.

"What—"

"It's water, honey. You need to calm down," Cyn said.

I tried to hand it back to her. "I don't need water."

Aidan sat next to me. "You just need to calm down. I won't let you drive if you're freaking out."

"My aunt just—"

"You're *shaking*, Bri. You need to calm down for my nephew," Kevin said.

"How can you be so calm?" I snapped. "She's your aunt too."

"What else am I supposed to do?" he asked. "I can't not be calm, Bri. Someone has to."

"Come here baby," Aidan said, pulling me into his arms. "I'll take you. You're not driving right now."

"But my car—"

"Will be safe," Aberlie said.

Aidan

I drove as fast as humanly possible to the hospital without causing a big wreck on the interstate. Briana tried getting a hold of John, who I guess was Lora's boyfriend, but she couldn't reach him. She didn't know exactly what happened and I think that started to drive her crazy. Kevin remained very quiet in the back of the car. We'd decided to take Briana's because we didn't know what kind of shape Lora was in and weren't sure how long she would have to be in the hospital.

John still wouldn't answer his phone.

That wasn't a good sign. I didn't want to tell Briana that though. She already freaked out bad enough as it was at Mom's. She didn't need to freak out anymore. It worried the hell out of me because the last thing we needed was for her to go into an early labor.

"I swear if he doesn't answer the damn phone then I'm going to choke him when we get inside," Bri said as soon as we pulled into the hospital parking lot.

"You'll choke him? I'll kick his ass," Kevin said.

"*Language.*"

"Listen, you both need to stay calm," I said.

I wasn't sure what I would do with those two. Lora tried to do as much as she could for them but she never was much of an aunt. If anything though she loved them both. Briana had a bad habit of beating herself up for things that were out of her control and I worried what she would do that when we got into the hospital and she finally calmed down. I didn't say it out loud, but *I* wanted to kick this John-Whatever's ass for the fact that my pregnant girlfriend had to go through this.

I hopped out of the car as soon as I cut the engine off. I'd tried calming them both down by playing some Beatles—I hadn't realized how crazy Bri was about them—but it didn't work. I worried what would happen if our son was a redhead, because if it was anything like his momma and uncle's tempers, we'd be stuck with a spoilt rotten hell demon. I just needed Bri to calm down. That's all I cared about, and all I told myself to worry about, because if I didn't I'd start thinking about how angry I was that this happened when things were going so well after I showed her the house.

Briana shot out of the car as fast as she could, which was pretty damn fast considering how big she'd gotten, Kevin not far behind her. I let them go on into the emergency room while I locked up the car and made sure to grab Bri's wallet—she'd insisted on bringing her purse but hadn't actually grabbed it. Poor thing let herself get in such a tizzy over her aunt, and it was understandable.

When I got inside of the hospital, Briana was hugging herself, talking to a woman who sat in one of the chairs in the waiting room.

"What happened?" Bri demanded.

"First of all, I am so sorry that your aunt was in that accident."

"Look, I get that you're the principal of the high school and everything, but I want to know what happened to my aunt. Where is she?"

"I really think you should wait to talk to one of the doctors, or the police—"

"Damn it!" Bri yelled. "I don't want to fucking wait. I want to know what happened to her!"

"Miss King?"

Bri whipped around. Two officers stood, their radios whizzing with background noise on their talkies while they tried to grab her attention. A doctor stood next to them, a grave looking man with a balding head. Kevin sat down, obviously not sure what to do in the situation. I stood there to support Bri, but mostly wanted to stay out of it unless she got so upset she started to have a panic attack again.

"Yeah," she said. "That's me."

"You might want to take a seat, ma'am."

The principal of the high school had tears running down her face and my immediate thought was *oh shit*. The look on Kevin's face told me he thought the same thing, and his eyes welled up. He sat down first.

"I refuse to sit down or be treated like I'm fragile just because I'm eight months pregnant," Briana said. "Tell me what's going on with my aunt."

"Your aunt was caught drinking on school property," the first cop said, the more serious looking one of the two. Not knowing what else to do because she *wouldn't* sit, I grabbed Bri's hand. "She was asked to leave the premises of the school at the end of the day and so she called her boyfriend, who came to pick her up. We believe the two of them got into an argument when she stole her keys back and got into her own vehicle. She pulled out of the entrance of the bus lane."

"Oh god," Bri said, tightening her grip on my hand, her voice breaking. "Are they—there weren't any kids on—?"

"No," the other cop said. "There were no children on the bus. Did you know your aunt had a drinking problem?"

"I—I did, but I never thought *this* would happen."

Kevin wiped his face off. "Is John—"

"He's currently in jail for something we found on his person," the serious cop said.

Bri whipped around to the doctor. "Where is my aunt? I need to see her. Please let me see her."

"I'm sorry, ma'am," the doctor said.

Oh hell, I thought to myself, sinking down to Bri's. I released her hand then wrapped my arms around her, hugging her from behind.

"We just lost her a few minutes ago…"

Bri simply turned around, wrapped her arms around me, and sobbed.

Chapter Fifteen

Aidan

Briana did nothing but sleep for two days straight after I got her and Kevin home. The home that was Lora's. With so much going on, Bri hadn't wanted to go back to the ranch just yet, and I didn't blame her. She wanted to move out. I was still making plans to get everything moved into the house. Samantha and Cyn took over making sure the house got painted and ready so I could stay with Bri and Kevin. This would only be until after the funeral arrangements were made and so Bri's grandfather could get out here. Turns out he was the co-signer for the original mortgage, so he'd decided to come stay in Tennessee until he could find a buyer for the house. I'd heard most of this by listening to phone conversations between Mr. King and Kevin.

"Mom, Bri is scaring the hell out of me," I said Thursday morning.

"Why?" she asked, looking up from the phone book in her lap. She sat with her legs folded in a kitchen chair. "She just seems tired."

I didn't answer at first, instead bypassing the chair Mom scooted out for me in favor of coffee. I scrubbed my hand over my face and realized I needed to shave.

"I know," I finally said, "it just seems like she's *too* tired."

I sat down with my coffee. Mom flipped through a few pages in the phone book and sipped her own drink. She had her hair down today, something I rarely saw her do anymore.

"What else do you expect, Aidan? She just lost her aunt." She flipped through a few more pages in the book. "I'm surprised she is handling this so well."

"She pushed her doctor's appointment back."

"I think that's reasonable," Mom said. "Has she had any more swelling?"

I took a drink of my coffee, thinking back to the last few days. Bri hadn't argued with me much when I laid in bed next to her and held her right after we got back from the hospital. I'd wanted to talk more about moving in together in order to try to distract her, but she mostly wanted to sleep. We hadn't touched each other. I was fine with that. It felt, to me, like we were redeveloping our emotional connection, and we needed that more than we needed sex right now, especially with her being eight months pregnant.

"No," I said. "She's been careful." Then I

sighed. "I just hate seeing her like this."

"Like what?"

Mom and I turned our heads to see Briana pad into the kitchen, a pair of loose sweats and an oversized t-shirt unable to hide the proof of her growing belly. Her hair had grown longer these past months and hung to the side in a messy braid.

I fell a little more in love with her.

"It's nothing," I said when both Mom and Bri looked at me funny. I cleared my throat and took a large gulp of coffee to mask my embarrassment.

Bri gave me a strange look then shrugged her shoulders and rolled her neck. "I feel like I've been sleeping too much. I have a headache."

"Do you want me to make you some tea?" Mom offered. "I should have put a pot on already."

"That would be great," Bri said, resting a hand on her stomach. She stared at me for a few seconds before she padded over to the table and pulled a chair out, sitting next to me. "I miss coffee."

"You could always have some decaf?" I suggested.

"Ew!" Bri said, fake-shuddering at my suggestion. "What's the point of drinking coffee if it's half-caff or decaf? No. I'd rather have tea or water."

I chuckled at her. "All right."

Mom laughed too, standing and walking to the stove. She made herself busy grabbing the coffee pot on the stove and filling it while Briana and I awkwardly looked at each other. I wanted to say something to her, anything, but a lot of what I wanted to say was something I didn't want to talk about in front of my mother.

"So," Aberlie said, breaking the awkward silence. "I'm glad you're awake. I actually needed to ask you a few questions about planning Lora's funeral, Bri."

"Oh," Bri said. She heavily eyed my coffee. "I was kind of hoping I could avoid that for like, ever."

Mom turned and gave Bri an admonishing look. "I told you I would take care of this for you but I can't do everything. Lora was still your aunt."

Bri sighed and rested her hands together on the kitchen table. "I feel like I shouldn't have any right to plan this for her."

I placed one of my hands over hers. "What do you mean? She was your aunt. Of course you have a right to make decisions about her funeral."

"She wanted to kick me out of her house before she died. I definitely shouldn't get a say! She was drinking too much, but I should have tried a gentler approach—they have things like free counseling down here, right? I should have tried to get her to go into some kind of rehab program."

"Hey," Mom said, sitting down again. "You can't blame yourself for getting mad at her. I would have been angry too."

"I just feel like the both of us handled everything so wrong."

I scooted my chair closer to her and wrapped my arms around her. Mom and I remained quiet while she sobbed, and I tried my best to soothe her while she cried. Briana clutched onto my shirt like her life depended on it and it made me feel like a dick, but I felt good to feel needed by her again. It was amazing to know Briana still needed me this way. Eventually

she ended up in my lap crying and I held her,
thankful that her brother wasn't there to see her cry
like this. It was bad enough that I had to order him to
go to school this morning.

I figured I'd make a decent dad if I could get
him to go to school without too much yelling at each
other. But staying in the house where Kevin acted
like I stepped all over his territory wasn't comfortable.

"Oh geez," Briana said, sitting up. She
whipped her face off. "Look at this." She hooked a
finger underneath the collar of my soaked t-shirt.
"Why do I always cry and ruin your clothes?"

I pushed her hair back. "It's okay. You're
allowed to cry."

She surprised me by hugging me. She
wrapped both arms around my neck and squeezed.
The teapot started whistling and Mom gave me a
gentle smile; seeing the two of us get along meant
something to her, I guess. She'd been a little worried
about how things would go the past few days.

We hadn't spoken about it with words but I
could sense that this situation was stressful to my
mother. We didn't need to talk to each other to know
that I worried like hell that Lora's death might force
Bri to make a final decision to move back to Kentucky.

"I don't know what I'd do without you guys."

"If you disentangle yourself from my son I'll
give you your tea," Mom laughed.

"Oh," Bri said, turning red. I could have killed
my mother for embarrassing her even though it was
adorable.

"I missed that blush," I said, taking her hand
and kissing it.

If possible, she turned redder and moved back to her original chair.

"Lilies, by the way," Briana said to Mom. "Lora loved lilies, and orchids."

Briana

Time sort of flew for me between making arrangements for Lora's funeral and getting things in order. I called my grandfather to confirm all the plans we'd made since I would not be staying in the house.

I stood next to my grandfather at the wake, Kevin scuffing his feet against the carpet next to us. We decided to have the wake at the house. Why do funerals always have to be so depressing?

Lora didn't have a will so I didn't know what to do. There were so many things she didn't do. She had very little savings and she hadn't paid the house off yet.

"What are you thinking about, sweetheart?"

I rested my head against Grandpa's shoulder and sighed when he pulled me into a side hug. "Lora left so many things behind that I don't know where to start."

Grandpa looked at my stomach. He'd been doing that a lot since he got to the church for the funeral. I hadn't wanted to have one there but Aberlie insisted and I finally gave in because Aberlie was kind enough to offer to help my grandfather pay for the funeral costs. I'd tried to argue with her on that but then she was helping me without asking for anything in return; how could I say no to that when I barely felt like I could keep my head above water since all of this happened?

"Did you know she was about to lose the house to the bank?" I asked.

"Yes," he said. "She called me as soon as she found out. I was a cosigner on the loan when she bought the house. I wouldn't have let that happen.

"Even so... I never thought it was so possible for her to be so irresponsible."

"Isn't that the pot calling the kettle black, sweetie?"

My eyes widened as I stared at my grandfather. "What do you mean?"

"Who's the father of that baby?" he asked, pointing to my stomach. "I thought I could trust you more than this."

I stepped away from my grandfather, unable to believe he would actually say something like that to me. I felt the first twinge of something tightening in my belly, but I decided to ignore it. My doctor warned me that I might start to feel Braxton Hicks contractions. I'd felt them a few times that day, and I was determined not to let them throw me off guard. I shouldn't have had to be on my guard around Grandpa, but I guess he had other thoughts on the issue.

"I'm the father," Aidan said, stepping beside me. He handed me a glass of water and ran a hand down my back. "Is something wrong, Bri?"

"There is something wrong, young man. Are you planning on marrying my granddaughter?"

"Grandpa," Kevin said. "Chill. Briana is an adult."

My grandfather glared at Kevin. "You have no room to talk either, young man, almost getting expelled from your last school in Kentucky."

"Who the hell do you think you are?" Kevin asked. "Whatever. Even with all the shit that is going on I still have homework to do. I'm going to my room."

Never in my life had I been so insulted.

"Actually—" Aidan started, but I waved him off. He didn't need to explain himself to my grandfather.

"No, don't," I said to him in warning. I looked up at my grandfather, who even though he had shrunk a little since I last saw him, still towered over me at five foot nine. "Grandpa, I appreciate your concern over me but I am fine. I can take care of myself."

"You're—"

"No," I said, holding my hands up. "I'm not doing this right now. I need something to eat since I feel dizzy. I'll talk to you about this later but not if you're going to come to the house and attack me for my decisions." I turned to Aidan. "Come with me to the kitchen?"

"Yeah, of course," he said, following me.

I didn't look back at my grandfather. I'm sure that pissed me off. I heard him start to say something but then one of Lora's former coworkers from the high school jumped in to talk to him.

"Are you okay?"

I warily looked in the direction of my grandfather, peaking outside of the kitchen. The next fake contraction felt stronger but I forced myself to brush it off even though I wanted to grab the counter.

"I think I just need to avoid him until it's time for him to leave."

"He's not staying with you?"

"No," I said, laughing. "Are you serious? He's not going to stay. He thinks this place is a dump. One guess who was his favorite kid when Dad and Lora were both still here?"

"That's shitty," Aidan said, opening up a bottle of sparkling grape juice and pouring himself a glass. I thought it would be a bad idea to serve alcohol at Lora's wake when that was how she died.

I groaned at the thought and reached down to try to get my shoes off. Whatever possessed me to wear kitten heels when I was eight months pregnant? I would never be able to explain it.

"I hate getting fat," I huffed. "Your child is making me fat." I couldn't get the damn shoes off.

Aidan laughed. I glared. He laughed harder.

"This isn't funny," I said, holding up one of my feet. "I'm a whale."

"You aren't even nine months pregnant yet. You're not fat." He took the shoe off and handed it to me.

Mistake.

"Oh!" I tossed a shoe at him. The son of a bitch ducked it and the shoe flew into a bunt cake that my cousin-something who I never met from Strongsville, Ohio, brought. "You suck!"

Aidan smirked at me and took my shoe out of the cake. The bottom of the shoe hadn't landed, but the top of it. He took a piece of the cake off my shoe and popped it into his mouth.

"That's not bad," Aidan said. "I wonder why

people always insist on bringing food to funerals."

"You are so disgusting," I said to him, unable to believe he just did that.

"You know you don't mean that."

"Cake? Off my shoe?"

"You forgot you're mad at me though, didn't you?"

I couldn't help it. I cracked a smile at him and shook my head. I felt wobbly walking on the foot that still had the other shoe, but I took it back from him and then kicked the other one off.

"Eat desserts off shoes when you're not around me. You might trigger my morning sickness all over again and I will never forgive you if you do."

"This is a horrible time to ask you this, but you can have your job back at the ranch?"

My heart pounded against my rib cage.

"You're right, this is a *horrible* time to have this conversation." I tossed kicked my shoes underneath the table.

"Come work back on the ranch," Aidan said.

I looked at my stomach and raised an eyebrow at him. "I'm pretty sure I won't be very useful right now."

"Mom could use some help with the more boring side of things, like the finances."

"I guess I could try to help her. I need to do something else for an income until I can go back to school."

"Oh," Aidan said, bending down to kiss my temple, "you're going back to school in August."

"What? How am I going to do that with a newborn?"

"He's got an uncle, grandparents, and his daddy. He'll be fine, baby."

"Come on, Cynthia!" Lee said, following her into the kitchen with Nikki hot on his trail. "I've told you I'm sorry. How many times do I have to apologize to you?"

When the hell did Nikki and Lee get there? I knew Nikki told me she was thinking about coming but I didn't actually expect her to come, and especially not with Lee. What was she thinking? I didn't think I'd have to tell her my aunt's wake would have to be a drama-free zone; that should have been a given, right?

"I'm sorry, where do I get a say in any of this?" Nikki said.

"Fuck you, Nikki," Cynthia said. "You aren't the one who was engaged to him."

"I'm not the one who made him second guess himself because I used him to cheat on my ex-boyfriend."

"Girls," Lee said, looking panicked. "Can we try to have a little more—?"

"Never have I touched a man who was in a loving relationship," Cynthia said. "I'm not that much of a whore."

"Hey!" Aidan roared, stepping away from me. "What the hell is going on?"

I could feel my blood pressure rising. I backed up to give everyone more space. Another pain ripped through and I grabbed the counter, reminding myself to breathe.

"How the fuck did you ever have a relationship with two women?" Lee asked, scratching his head in confusion. "I don't know how you ever did it. These two are driving me insane!"

"You're an asshole!" Cynthia said, bursting into tears. "I was willing to spend the rest of my life with you and you couldn't take me seriously? You are the lowest piece of—"

I couldn't take it. I couldn't stand the yelling. I turned around and grabbed the closest thing I could reach, a glass pan of lasagna, and threw it on the ground. It shattered everywhere and made everyone look at me.

"OUT!" I said. "Just get out of here. Cynthia, Nikki, I love the both of you but I swear if you don't get out of this house you're going to regret it! How *dare* you start a fight like this at my aunt's wake?"

I burst into tears, unable to keep it together anymore.

Grandpa came barreling into the kitchen himself.

Contractions. I'd started having contractions, I was certain. This felt more serious than Braxton Hicks.

"What the hell is going on here?"

"You!" I said to him, pointing. "I want you to—ow, *son of a bitch*!" I gasped, grabbing for a chair. I needed to sit down. Something wet gushed down my leg.

"What on earth—Bri!"

Aberlie and Aidan both rushed to me at the same time. I sucked in a deep breath, tears welling up in my eyes at the pain. It definitely felt like labor, oh hell.

"I—I can't be in labor. It's too early. Like—um...FUCK. I don't know. It's early!"

Kevin skidded on his feet next to me. "What—oh that's *gross*."

"Well, is everyone just going to stand there?" Aberlie barked. "Get off your asses and help her to the car!"

Chapter Sixteen

Aidan

I needed to take a minute.

I wanted to punch Briana's doctor, so they told me to take a breather.

Fucking early labor.

She was having the baby today and there was nothing we could do to stop it.

They placed her at about thirty-five, thirty-six weeks or something. I wasn't sure. I'd heard the entire conversation but it all went by in a blur. She freaked out and threatened to choke the doctor if he didn't back off to let her breathe.

I couldn't help but be fucking proud of her. She wouldn't let them give her an epidural or go the easy route with a caesarian section that the fucking doctor tried to bully—no, *offered*, it was a safer route because the baby's heartbeat was a little fast. Briana said no, and I nearly punched him. Our son would be fine. He'd need some time in the NICU, I guessed, but he'd be fine.

Bri demanded space from everyone. Couldn't blame her. She had just gotten a few ice chips when I finally decided to leave for a minute so I could give everyone an update.

"Is she okay?" Mom said, firing off the first round of questions as soon as I reached the waiting room.

"She's having him today."

Cynthia sat curled up in a ball as far away as she could get from Nikki and Lee. Lee paced back and forth in front of a few chairs not far from some vending machines.

"Tell her she's a badass," Kevin said.

A few more people said a few things to me. I guess a few guests from the wake trailed in to make sure she was okay, but now she was leaving. An irritated nurse who looked like she'd sucked on too much prune juice sat behind a desk, glaring at every single one of us. All of that shit faded though as soon as I saw my cousin.

Next thing I know, I walked up to him.

"Hey, Lee," I said.

"Hey, man, is she okay—?"

Bam. Right in the nose. Blood spewed out onto the floor, Mom and Lee yelped, and Nikki shrieked and jumped back.

"*Aidan!*" With a force greater than I expected from my mother, she yanked me back. "What the hell has gotten into you, son?"

"Because Lee is an asshole, a big fucking fight

broke out in the kitchen. What the hell were the three of you thinking?"

"Hey, what did I do that was wrong?" Cyn said, tears welling up in her eyes. "I didn't ask for them to show up."

"You *know* better, Cynthia! Hell, I'd hope that you would know better than anyone! Bri has been stressed out since Lora died. It's been an awful week and I just—"

My voice broke a little. Fuck. This was way too hard to handle emotionally.

"I can't deal with this right now," I said. Several people tried to get me to stop but I didn't listen to them, instead going back in the direction I'd come from. I wanted to check on Briana. *Needed* to check on her.

Briana

I sat next to Aidan, staring at our perfect son in my arms.

"I'm never giving birth again."

He laughed, wrapping his arm around me.

"I can't believe you actually decided to give birth without anything."

"I'm tough."

He leaned over and kissed my head. "You are."

"I'm just glad everything is okay." I sighed in relief, staring down at him.

"I think I freaked out on everyone earlier."

I raised an eyebrow, looking up at Aidan. "You did?"

"Because you went into labor early."

"I was almost full term." I stared at every inch of our son before I spoke again. They'd been worried he might need a little extra attention when he was born, but everything seemed fine. His vitals were strong. He was every bit of six pounds and might have been bigger had I actually gotten to the due date. "Why'd you have to go and be stubborn and be born today?"

"Hey," Aidan said, wiping some tears from my cheek. "What's wrong?"

"I just wish Lora was here."

"Oh baby, I'm sorry."

I shook my head and scooted over. "Climb up here. We need to name him."

"You haven't picked one out yet?"

I shook my head. "For some reason I just couldn't bring myself to think about names. I think it's because it was something I was supposed to do with you, but I was being too stubborn, so I just never thought about it."

Aidan grinned at me then kissed my cheek before he carefully climbed onto the bed. The baby cooed and tried to wiggle but he was wrapped up tight in a blue blanket. I'd been about to wallop one of the nurses until they finally decided to let us have some time alone.

"So, how about Alex?"

"Veto."

Aidan rolled his eyes. He didn't need to ask. I had as much veto power as I wanted even though I wanted to let him name our son.

"Joshua."

"No way. Too biblical. Veto."

"I like that name—"

"*Veto.*"

"Fine. Aaron? David? Hell, we'll name him Adam!"

"Veto, veto, and veto," I said, groaning. "Come on, I know you're better at coming up with names."

"Naming a thoroughbred is different than naming my son."

"Fine…Edgar, last try."

"*NO!*" I shrieked. "I know you love your literature, but our kid isn't getting named after Edgar Allen Poe."

~*~

Cynthia

(Yeah, you're reading that right.)

William Franklin Aidan McCoy.

That's what Bri and Aidan were talking about when I left the hospital, anyway. I guess his middle name was still up for debate, like that Bri wanted to add all those names, but Aidan was convinced they would confuse the poor kid. She'd insisted on naming him after their dads and having Aidan's name in there somewhere. I had to laugh when I heard that because Briana couldn't be a normal person and just name the poor kid Aidan Jr.

"Cynthia, we need to talk about this."

I tensed up in Lee's car. I'd gone crazy when I decided to take his offered ride home. No one needed us there when I decided to. Nikki stayed behind because she wanted to see the baby and apologize to Bri, I guess.

I couldn't...

I couldn't stay there.

Seeing little William Franklin Aidan McCoy reminded me too much of the baby I might have had, had I decided not to terminate my pregnancy. Since she went into labor I'd constantly felt like crying. At least I wasn't having a panic attack yet. I might, though, if I didn't get out of Lee's car soon.

"There's nothing to talk about," I said, opening the car door. I didn't even care that we'd just gotten into town and that we weren't anywhere near my apartment yet. We were close to campus. That was far enough.

"What the hell are you doing?" he asked.

"What's it look like I'm doing?" I asked, unbuckling my seatbelt. "I'm getting out of the damn car."

"I'm sorry I fucked up, but—"

I didn't listen to him. I'd almost gotten my freedom before someone honked the horn. I smacked Lee when he reached over me, yanked my foot back into the car, and slammed the door shut.

"Do I have to throw your ass in the back seat where there are child locks?" Lee asked, stopping at the stop sign.

"Fuck you."

"As much as I'd love to, baby, we need to talk a few things out."

Damn. He started driving again. I flushed red at the thought of having sex with Lee *ever* again, then became angrier. He had no right to treat me the way he did. To propose to me; to make me think he actually wanted me to be his wife. Now I knew what drove women bat shit crazy enough to hurt their significant other. I *wanted* to hurt him. I thought about slamming my hand down onto his balls.

"You're crying."

"No shit, Sherlock," I hissed at him, wiping my face.

"I don't know why me sleeping with Nikki is such a big deal. You slept around on Aidan all the time. Pretty sure you messed around with someone else when you were dating him *and* me, too."

"Just keep driving, Lee."

"You won't even consider talking to me?"

I looked at him. *Really* looked at him. Lee and Aidan were different as night and day. Aidan had always been a solid, grounded man. A hard working man. He hardly ever lost his head unless it came to his lover, actually. Lee was way different. He picked fights in bars, skipped days for work because Aberlie let him get away with it, and didn't understand why I got bent out of shape when he wanted to do things like cheat on me and move back the wedding. I should have known from the start that I made a mistake when I started sleeping with him. It hurt; physically hurt, to see Aidan and Briana today with their new son.

I'd been sure my heart got ripped out when we both decided things were over, but I'd been so wrong.

"Go jump off a bridge, Lee."

I escaped the car at the next red light, not bothering to turn back when Lee yelled for me. This time, the light had been in front of campus, and I quickly made myself lost amongst the crowd of other students.

ABOUT THE AUTHOR

I wrote in a previous "about the author" that I'm vegetarian. I struggle with this a lot, but more importantly, I still feel animals should be treated with the utmost respect. That's part of the reason I started the Over series.

I live in Irvine, Kentucky with my mom, and I work in a call center to afford my beautiful covers by my designer. I'm a proud animal mom to two bunnies and a small flock of chickens.

I LOVE to connect with readers. If you would like, you may follow me here:

Twitter: @mara_a_miller
Instagram: maram1986
Facebook:
https://www.facebook.com/maraamillerfiction
Blog:www.maraamillerfiction.blogspot.com

Cheap Lies

The *Cheap* Series

A Short Prequel

Coming Soon

Prologue

Take a *chill pill*.

Gwen threw the lid from her bottle of Sailor Jerry's onto the coffee table next to the small bag of Valium. She stared at the bag, shook her head, and poured herself three shots into her brother's set novelty *Star Wars* shot glasses.

Brandon had *no* idea how much she wanted those pills.

She knocked back her first drink.

It would be easy for her. She did it all the time before when she needed to calm her nerves while she still lived in New York. She *depended* on those tiny white pills once, and it would be no problem for her to start again.

Ignore *everything*, including the pills, she told herself. She didn't need either. What she *wanted* to do was to relax and enjoy her time alone in the house, something not easily done when she lived with her younger brother and her daughter.

Jay: Baby, I'm coming back home.

Gwen: No, ur not.

Jay: Don't u love me?

"Screw this," Gwen said. She threw her phone. It landed somewhere on the floor next to the coffee table.

Gwen told Jay to stop sending text messages and to stop calling her. He never quite grasped that she sometimes needed time to herself. She couldn't get him to understand why they ended their relationship. It made her sick to her stomach.

Jay finally needed to know the truth, but she didn't know how to without his anger getting the best of him. He couldn't come back to Kentucky. Since he left, it was like she could finally breathe. Gwen had her freedom back. Amy was happier, and so was she. If Jay finally knew the truth about Amy's birth certificate then maybe he could move on. That is, *if* he didn't turn into a raging bipolar asshole.

Gwen sadly expected nothing less from him.

Loud, frantic knocking made her spill her fucking drink.

"Fuck!" she yelled, standing.

The knocking continued. Gwen didn't want to answer the door. She *told* everyone not to bother her. Neal respected her wishes. Brandon tried calling her, but she couldn't stand him and his drama with Elise any longer. That's when she kicked him out of his own house. Neal, their younger brother, at least had the decency to know when she needed an adult time-out; one that included a lot of soap opera binging and drinking.

No one knew about the pills.

"Who is it!?" she yelled, not the least bit sorry for her bitchy tone of voice.

"Charlie!"

Shit.

Gwen quickly grabbed the pills and stuffed them in her bra. Why the hell had Charlie decided to show up? They hardly talked much anymore. He barely looked at her whenever she worked at the auto shop and usually barked orders about whatever he needed like some kind of Neanderthal.

"What?"

"Whoa," Charlie said. "Brandon wasn't kidding when he said you're in a bad mood."

"And you think pointing this out to me right away is a good reason why...?" she asked.

Charlie hardly aged a day in the past six years. If anything, being out of the army softened him up, but he still had thick, muscled arms. Gwen would willingly bet her next paycheck from the auto shop that he still had a six pack too. He wore his hat from the army now and bits of his brown hair rebelliously escaped. He no longer wore the buzz cut. Gwen almost wished he would because that might make him less appealing, she thought, as she looked up at him. He stood a solid six feet compared to her tiny five-foot-four and ass that didn't seem to want to relinquish the baby fat.

He took the hat off and shuffled his feet. Gwen couldn't remember a time she ever saw Charlie get nervous, but his hair had gotten too long, and slid through his fingers like butter. She wondered what he would do if she ran her fingers through it. Was it really soft like she thought?

"I want to talk."

"I've lived back in Kentucky way longer than you have," Gwen said, unwilling to tone down her snark. "You barely say five words to me unless it's to bark orders about ordering a part for a car."

"I—I know that."

Stammering? Gwen thought. Her shoulder dropped; she hadn't realized how stiffly she stood in the entrance.

"What's up, Charlie?"

"I've been thinking," he said. "Brandon and Elise keep acting like morons, but *I* keep wondering if we aren't doing the exact thing."

"*No*," Gwen said. "Don't go there."

"Gwen, I'm in love with you."

She slammed the door in his face.

Please, if you liked this book, share it. Share it *everywhere*! I'm an independent author and rely solely on Twitter, Facebook, and Instagram, and my blog to advertise my work. I'm *still* learning how to do all of this too. I am working in the direction of getting a website set up. I LOVE email, and I LOVE conversing with my readers. You can email me at mara_a_miller@hotmail.com, go to the links in my "about the author" to find me on my social media, and locate me on Good Reads. Sometimes on my blog, I'll post excerpts of what I've been writing. I'm in the process of gathering together contacts for a mailing list as well.

Made in the USA
Columbia, SC
23 February 2021